What's best for you

Books by Judie Angell

In Summertime It's Tuffy

Ronnie and Rosey

Tina Gogo

A Word from Our Sponsor
or My Friend Alfred

Secret Selves

Dear Lola
or How to Build Your Own Family

What's Best for You

BRADBURY PRESS   SCARSDALE, NEW YORK

What's best for you

A novel by Judie Angell

Library of Congress Cataloging in Publication Data
Angell, Judie. What's best for you.
Summary: Three children try to adjust to a new life after their parents
divorce.
  [1. Divorce—Fiction. 2. Single-parent families—Fiction] I. Title.
PZ7.A5824Wh   [Fic]   80-27425
ISBN 0-87888-181-6

This is for David, Lynn and Ruth

What's best for you

One

The trunk was three-quarters packed. It stood open in the middle of the braided rug in Lee's room, surrounded by piles of shirts, jeans, shorts, bathing suits and underwear. Lee knew she'd never fit everything in but decided she'd give it all she had and then use cartons for the rest. She put a folded pile of tee shirts into the trunk, stepped back and looked around. The top shelf was missing.

Wondering how she could lose a whole top shelf of a trunk, she began to dig angrily among the piles of clothing on the floor. It wasn't there and suddenly she wanted to cry. She took a deep breath and threw herself across her bed. The shelf, made of stiff blue cardboard, was lying on the floor between the bed and the window.

Still on her stomach, Lee reached out to touch the cardboard. It was faded, even torn in spots. She rubbed her fingers along the edge. It had been her camp trunk. Years ago. About a hundred years ago, Lee thought.

Near tears again, she rolled over, sat up and in one swift movement, reached her dresser. She opened the bottom drawer and saw all her sweaters, folded neatly in plastic bags.

She slammed the drawer shut and whirled around, leaning heavily against the dresser. She ran her tongue across her upper lip. Then she strode across the room toward the door, kicking clothes out of her way with her foot.

Lee's mother was on the floor in the kitchen, wrapping plates in newspaper and putting them neatly in cardboard cartons. She looked up at the sound of her daughter's heavy step.

"Hi," she said and blew a strand of hair off her forehead. "How are you doing?"

Lee was panting a little but she tried to sound casual. "Listen, I've decided to take my sweaters," she said. "And my wool skirts."

Her mother didn't answer, merely looked up at her.

"*All* my clothes. Everything. I might as well," Lee said, defiantly now.

Her mother stood up and pushed the same strand of hair off her face with her hand.

"That's silly, Lee," she said softly. "Not only won't you need them, your father doesn't even have room for them in that small apartment of his. We decided to store all our winter things in the cedar closets in the basement here. There's plenty of room."

"What if the tenants want to use those closets?" Lee pouted. "Besides, I want to feel settled. If I'm going to be living with Daddy I want all my things with me. All of them."

"Stop it, Lee," her mother said calmly. "In the fall, when you come to me, we'll pick up all your winter things and you'll have everything you need. Then we'll be able to store your summer things—"

"Why can't I just keep everything together!" Lee's words came out a shriek and brought her younger sister, Allison, into the kitchen. Allison had a tentative smile on her face. Peace was needed and, as she had done for years, Allison would make it.

"Hey," she began, "I thought you guys were packing . . ."

"I'm trying to explain," Lee said, "that I want all my things with me, not just summer stuff."

"Why?" Allison's eyes widened. "You're only going to be at Daddy's for the summer."

"That's what I was saying," their mother said.

"I just want it all, what's wrong with that, why do you have to give me a hard time about everything!" Lee cried.

"Come on, Lee . . ." Allison touched her sister's arm. "Come on. It doesn't make any difference . . . You'll have everything when you need it . . . Please don't fight now, this is our last night . . ."

Their last night in their house. Allison couldn't finish, she couldn't say it.

Lee clicked her tongue and looked away from both of them.

"Please?" Allison said and smiled, first at Lee, who wasn't looking, then at their mother.

"We won't fight, Allison," their mother said and sighed.

Allison nodded hesitantly and left the kitchen. Her room was at the head of the stairs. She had her own packing to finish but she opened her door wider, ready to rush down again at the slightest sound of discord.

"Why do you do this, Lee?" her mother asked wearily after Allison had left. "You're fifteen years old, your sister's only twelve, and she has more sense of how to behave than—"

"Let's hear all about it," Lee said, rolling her eyes.

Her mother sighed. No matter what she said, Lee seemed to take it badly. She felt an urge to grab her daughter and shake her but at the same time to hold her tightly. Straightening her shoulders, she tried a different tack. "You know," she said, looking right into Lee's eyes, "if you wanted to pack all your sweaters, slacks, skirts, knee socks—whatever—you could have just buried them in boxes and not said a word to me. Couldn't you?"

Lee didn't say anything. She looked at the floor.

"Couldn't you?" her mother repeated. "You didn't

have to make the announcement that you were taking all your winter things to your father's when you're going to spend only the summer there. You did it just to pick another argument with me, didn't you?"

"No," Lee said.

"Yes, you did. You knew what I would say but you came in here and started it anyway."

"How was I supposed to know what you were going to say?" Lee asked defiantly.

"Oh, Lee . . . Because we've all talked about it so much. About the plans, the things we agreed upon . . . We all decided you'd stay with your dad for the summer and then in the fall, come in to us when school starts and we'd be together again. So why would you bring your winter things to your father's when you'll be in New York in the wintertime? That's what you knew I'd say . . ."

Lee looked up angrily. "Well, *I'm* not the one who got a divorce," she said. "It's not *my* fault all these new arrangements have to be made."

Her mother jabbed a forefinger at her. "Now don't you pull that on me, young lady!" she said. "Your starting arguments with me—deliberately starting them—didn't begin with the divorce *or* the separation! You have been doing this to me for years now, taking every one of your worries and frustrations out on me! Now I can take it and even understand it up to a point, but—"

"Oh, yes," Lee said, "you're so understanding! Is that why you criticize everything I do? My hair, my clothes, my behavior—"

She stopped as Allison appeared again in the kitchen doorway. Behind her was their seven-year-old brother, Joel. He was frowning worriedly. "Um . . ." Allison began, putting a hand on Joel's shoulder, ". . . I need your help, Lee—I can't find my black suitcase . . ."

Their mother had begun to cry. Joel tugged on the end of Allison's string belt and Allison went to her quickly. "It's okay," she murmured. "Don't cry, Mom. We're all uptight, don't take it seriously, Lee didn't mean it . . ."

Their mother sniffled and tried to hide her face as she reached for a tissue on the kitchen counter. "Sorry," she said softly.

"I didn't mean it, I'm sorry," Lee said in one breath and pushed Allison toward the door. As she stepped out of the room she turned back. Her mother was leaning over the sink, her head down. "I'm sorry," Lee said again and quickly started for the stairs.

The next morning Joel sat on his bed, stripped now of sheets and blankets, and looked around the room which wouldn't be his much longer. Even last night, with all the packing, it hadn't seemed real—it hadn't seemed that he'd be leaving it for good . . .

Most of the boxes with his clothes and toys had

already been brought downstairs that morning. Bit by bit, everything that was Joel was moving out of his room.

Downstairs, he could hear his mother calling. But she wasn't calling him. Not yet. He could stay a little while longer. He could get his secret box out from under his bed, where he'd kept it until the last minute, and look through all his most personal things again . . .

"Allison . . . Allison!" Their mother turned from the foot of the stairs and bumped into Lee. The two of them stepped away from each other with exasperated looks. Neither said "Watch where you're going" as both had been immediately tempted to do. "Lee, have you seen your sister?" her mother asked.

"No, Mother." She said it politely.

"Do you think you can stop what you're doing long enough to find her for me? There are some things she has to go through before I pack them."

Lee sighed. "Daddy'll be here any minute . . ."

"I know, but you can take one moment—" She stopped as the front doorbell rang.

"That's Daddy!" Lee cried and ran to the door. They had been so busy with the end of school and packing, she hadn't seen him for three days, though his apartment was within biking distance for her.

It wasn't her father at the door. It was a stocky man wearing a green jump suit and cap.

"Currie?" the man grunted.

"Yes," Lee said.

"Repp's Moving," the man said.

"Oh! Come in!" her mother called.

The man turned and nodded toward his truck, parked outside at the curb. Another man in green climbed out and came toward him.

"You're right on time," Lee's mother told them, smiling nervously. "I didn't expect that . . . I mean, no one ever comes when they say they will . . ." Still wearing the smile, she took them into the living room. "The things I want to be moved are tagged. The rest stays here," she said.

The men nodded and picked up a swivel rocker.

"Doesn't Daddy want that?" Lee asked, turning to her mother.

"No, he could have taken it six months ago if he'd wanted it."

"Well, it wasn't so final until now," Lee said.

Her mother sighed. "Lee, your father's apartment is furnished. He doesn't need this chair and if he does he can always have it and he knows it. Please don't start." She hurried on, "I asked you to please find your sister, I really do need her, especially now the movers are here."

Lee turned and stomped up the stairs calling, "Allison!" in a halfhearted voice.

She found Allison in her room, sitting on her bed and staring at her dresser.

"Allie?"

"What?"

"Mother wants you to go through some things downstairs."

"Okay . . ."

"Are you all right?"

"Yes . . . When is Daddy coming for you?"

"Pretty soon . . . I'll miss you . . ." Lee smiled a tiny smile at her younger sister.

"I'll miss you, too," Allison said. "But we'll all be together when the summer's over, right?"

Lee shrugged. "All except Daddy . . ."

"*Allison!*" their mother cried from downstairs.

Allison jumped up. "I'm coming!" she called back and hurried out of the room.

Joel stood in the middle of his almost-bare room, turning his body helplessly around and around, squinting, searching . . . "Allison?" he called softly. He bent down and peered under his bed again, but the shaft of sunlight streaming from his window didn't reach far enough and he didn't know where his flashlight was now . . . "Allison!" he called louder. His throat hurt.

Lee appeared in his doorway. "She went downstairs, Joel. What's the matter?"

He looked up with tears in his eyes. "I can't find the key to my secret box," he said. The small metal filing box sat forlornly on his mattress.

"Why don't you just pack the box, Joelly," Lee suggested, "and then when you get to New York I'm sure you'll find the key. Or Mother can have one made for you. But look, the movers are here now so you better get going."

"Why aren't you coming, too, Lee?" Joel asked as he picked up his box.

"You know why, Joelly, I'm spending the summer with Daddy."

"Why?"

"Because I have a job here this summer. You know that, Joel . . ."

He looked down at the floor.

"Besides, all my friends are here . . ." she continued.

"All my friends are here, too," he said, still staring down.

Lee sat on Joel's bed and pulled him over to her. "Listen, Joelly . . . Mother is moving into New York. None of us is going to stay in this house any more. And you know it, so you have to stop thinking that things can be the way they used to be because they can't."

"Why do you get to stay?" he asked, not looking at her.

"I'm not staying here, I'm staying at Daddy's. And I'm older, so I can look after myself while Daddy's at work. And I'll be working, too. Listen: are you ever going to stop asking the same questions over and over?"

"I wish I didn't have to . . . go . . ." Joel said.

"Lee! Your father's here!"

Lee jumped up from the bed, dragging her brother by the wrist. "Come on, Joel, Daddy's here! Daddy's here!"

Their father was waiting at the foot of the stairs, smiling up at his children.

Lee grinned back. School had ended yesterday, the nineteenth of June, and now he had come for her. Summer was beginning.

"Hey, is that my big boy, hiding back there?" her father called, half-starting up the stairs.

Joel peeked around from a bend in the landing. "Hi, Daddy . . ."

"Well, come on down here!" their father called. "I can't pick you up on the stairs! Come on!"

Joel half-ran, half-fell down the rest of the stairs into his father's arms.

"Good to see you, buddy," his father whispered as he hugged him hard. He set Joel down and looked at Lee.

"You all set, toots? Where's your stuff?"

"All the boxes in the dining room are mine. Nobody else put anything in there," she told him.

"Hey, Joel, want to give me a hand with your sister's stuff?"

"No," Joel said.

Their father moved his lips together, back and forth. Then he knelt down and put his hands on Joel's waist. "It's going to be okay, son," he said. "I know it will."

Joel didn't answer.

"Come on, Joelly," Lee said, taking his hand. "Let's bring some things out to the car." They passed their mother on their way out. She had made herself even busier after their father's arrival, finding more to do in other rooms. Lee knew her mother was avoiding him, the way she always did when he'd dropped the kids off or picked them up or had *anything* to do at the house. But now she was approaching him, so Lee hurried into the dining room to avoid their conversation.

"Alan?"

"Hello, Elaine." He straightened up.

"There are still some things of yours . . . When I was packing, I—Is there anything you want?" She rested her arm on the newel post.

"Like what, summer things?" he asked.

"No . . . not summer. Heavy shirts. Corduroy slacks. I know you don't have a lot of room, but—"

He shook his head. "No," he answered, "I don't have the room. Can't you put them in the basement for me and I'll get them in the fall? Or will what's-their-name object?"

"Who?"

"You know. Your tenants."

The movers brushed by them on their way upstairs.

"No," she said, "they won't mind. We can store anything we want, as long as it's out of the way."

"Fine. Now I think we should get the children together . . . So we can discuss the schedule for the summer. Do you know where Allison is?"

"She was here with me a moment ago. I don't know now. I keep losing her . . ." She looked around and called. "Listen . . . There's nowhere for us to sit down. The movers are taking everything out . . ."

"I thought you were leaving it all furnished for the tenants."

"Well, it started out that way, but they've decided to bring more and more of their own things. The dining room. That's staying. Let's go in there. Oh! Allison—"

"Sorry, didn't mean to startle you, Mom. I thought I heard you call again."

Her mother's eyes met Allison's. She didn't have to look down at her any more. Why, her mother wondered, hadn't the fact struck her until this moment?

She touched Allison's face. "Yes. Yes, honey, your father and I want to talk to you. Would you go find your sister and brother and come on into the dining room? It's the only place where we can sit down . . ."

Lee and Joel were already there, each holding a cardboard box to take to their father's car.

"Put those down a second, kids," their father said. "And come sit with us."

Their mother pulled two chairs away from the table for them. She had caned them herself. She'd learned how in a course she took the year all the children were in school the whole day for the first time.

Allison was already seated and looking from one parent to the other.

"We wanted to talk to you," their mother began, "about how the visits back and forth will go this summer . . ."

Allison looked away from their faces.

"See, we thought it would be best—" their father touched the back of a cane chair and rocked it a little, "—if Joelly and Allison stayed in the city on weekends. Just in the beginning."

Their mother spoke and Joel and Lee shifted their gaze to her. "You see . . . it's really a new life for us. The new apartment, New York City, my schedule, yours . . . It's all different. And it's a lot to adjust to . . ."

"That's right," their father continued and now they looked at him. "We thought it would be good for you, Lee, to have some time by yourself with me. But—" he spoke directly to Allison, forcing her to look up, "—that doesn't mean we won't be seeing each other because I wouldn't be able to stand that. I'm in the city every day. You and Joel can come up to my office after you finish your camp and summer school activities . . . And at least one night a week I'll take you both out to dinner. Okay?"

Now Lee was the only one looking at her father.

"Okay, Joel? Okay, Allison?" he asked.

"We worked out this idea together," their mother interrupted, "because we really felt it would be the best way. And then when we're all adjusted, why, we'll just continue our regular weekend schedule of visits back and forth . . . Of course, Lee, I hope you come see us . . . without a schedule . . ."

And now Lee looked away.

"Well, how does that sound?" their father asked. "Just till everybody gets used to everything."

"We come up to your office?" Joel asked softly.

"You bet you do!" his father almost boomed. "Allison will pick you up from the camp bus after she's through with school—right?"

Allison nodded.

"And we'll go out for ice cream or sodas or something, whatever you'd like."

Their mother said, "Don't you think that'll be best? To have a more relaxed schedule this summer?"

Lee shrugged. Her mother was looking directly at her. "I guess," she mumbled.

"Allison?" her father said.

"It's all right," Allison said. "I can take care of Joel and it'll work out."

"Good girl. Of course it will," her father went on. "Okay with you Joelly?"

Joel nodded.

"Okay." Their parents exchanged glances. "Fine. Now we can finish loading the car."

15

Lee's father's living room had sliding glass doors which opened onto a small back yard. The apartments were new, built near the beach for all-year-round tenants, or summer weekenders. He'd taken a two-bedroom for all the times when the children stayed with him. If all three slept over at once he gave Joel the choice of sleeping with him, or alone in his room while he slept on the convertible couch in the living room.

The place had a good-sized kitchen and he liked that because he enjoyed cooking. He'd picked it up again when the children's mother had taken a job last year. Since January, when he was alone during the week, he usually ate out. Now Lee would be there every evening; he was looking forward to cooking for her. Having the children on weekends wasn't what he called "being a daddy"—able to share in their homework at night or listen to their everyday ups and downs. With Lee here for the summer, he thought, he could feel like a family man again, with something to show for sixteen years of marriage. He didn't miss the marriage any more and that fact sometimes surprised him. The differences between them had seemed to become more and more important—until only the differences remained.

"It's beautiful, Daddy!" Lee cried when they arrived at the apartment with her things.

"Well, thanks, but you've only seen it about a hundred times," he said, smiling.

"I know, but . . . now it's mine," she said, and smiled back.

"Yes," he said. "I look at it differently now, too." He put a large carton down in the hall. "Hey, you just going to stand there admiring the digs or do I get some help here?" he asked.

"Oh, sure. And then can I call Eileen?"

"Of course you may. This is your place, too, you know."

"I know, I know, I know!" she cried and bounced out to the car.

Lee dialed half of Eileen's number before she remembered that this was Eileen's weekend with her father, so she called Virginia. Virginia had been with her father the weekend before.

"Gin?" she cried happily when her friend came to the phone. "Guess where I am?"

"I give up. Paris?"

"No. Someplace just as good."

"Where, Lee?"

"I'm . . . home."

"Okay . . ."

"Come on, Gin, I'm here! At my dad's."

There was a gasp at the other end. "You're really there?"

"Yup!"

"Well, congratulations," Virginia said. "I really wasn't sure it would work out."

"I've been telling you, haven't I? Haven't I been packing all week?"

"Well, that's what you said . . . I thought you were secretly cramming for exams."

"I did that, too. Just knowing I was coming here made me work better."

"Boy, Lee, you're really lucky. None of our fathers could have us. I'm glad for you. But too jealous to stand it."

Lee giggled. "Thanks," she said.

Then Virginia added, "But it is only for the summer, isn't it?"

"Do me a favor, Virginia, don't say that."

"Sorry . . ."

"No, I mean it. It's just beginning and that's all I want to think about."

"I don't blame you. Want to get together today or tomorrow?"

"Can't," Lee answered. "I have to get unpacked. But we have next week before day camp starts. We'll go to the beach, okay?"

"Sure. I want to get a good tan before we start work. Look my best for all the cute boy counselors."

"You *hope* they're cute boy counselors!"

"I *hope!* Did your mom and the kids move today, too?"

"Yeah . . ."

"You still haven't seen that apartment, have you?"

Lee sighed. "Well, she hasn't even had it that long

and besides, there was so much to do with finals and packing—"

"Listen, you want some help over there? I haven't got much to do and my mom's going out."

"Thanks, but I—I just want to get used to being here," Lee answered.

Two

Hello, Mother, this is Lee. Surely you remember me, your daughter, Lenore Currie. That's right, so it does ring a bell, good, because I remember reading somewhere that most mothers like to maintain contact with their children at least until they reach the age of twenty-one!

Lee slid over from her desk chair onto her bed, put her hands behind her head and lay back on the pillow. It was a petit point pillow with an abstract design on it—one of three her mother had made for her room at the house when they'd redone it.

I mean, it has been four whole days since you moved, and it might interest you to know that your oldest child finished sixteenth in a class of two hundred and fifty-two ninth graders this year. And that she got a ninety-seven in her English exam. But probably not, Mother, because all your special graduate courses and your new life in New York City don't interest me in the slightest either, so that just about makes us even. Well, I'm glad we had this little chat, Mother. Goodbye and have a nice day!

"Grrr-ROW!" Lee growled out loud and rolled over onto her stomach.

"What?" she heard her father call from the kitchen.

"Nothing, I was just—"

"*What?*"

"*Nothing!*"

She picked up *Seventeen* magazine from the floor next to her bed and began to thumb through it. She yawned and stretched.

Hello, Mother?

"Lee! Where's the wok cookbook?" her father yelled.

"I thought you were using it!"

"I am, I mean the other one. The one with the photograph of vegetables on the cover!"

Lee smiled to herself and called back, "Daddy, that's about the last thing I'd ever be needing to use! I don't know where it—"

"It's okay, I got it!"

Lee hugged herself, still smiling. This was more than summer vacation; it was a vacation just to live with her father. If she hadn't picked up her room or hadn't done a chore or dressed sloppily, there was no nagging about it! Her father let her be! And if he ever did speak to her about anything, he only said it once. He didn't *harp*. *He* loves me the way I am, she thought. People should love people for exactly what they are and not try to change them . . .

But what if they're unlovable? Really unlovable.

I'm not.

I'm not.

She leaped off the bed and ran for the kitchen, where she stood in the doorway for two minutes before speaking.

"Daddy?"

He jumped. "Hey, you startled me, honey. I didn't even hear you come out of your room."

"Sorry. Daddy, what are my good qualities?"

He put down the cookbook and looked at her.

"Well!" he said with a half-smile. "I need some time for that one! I mean, I've really got to wrack my brain and—"

"No, please . . . I mean it," she said.

"You're bright, you have a great sense of humor . . . You're very sweet."

"I'm not sweet," she said seriously. "Allison's sweet. I'm not."

He scratched his head. "But you're kind. You care about people. You're wonderful with your sister. And your brother, too."

Lee shook her head. "No. Allison's good with Joel. I hardly ever have anything to do with Joel."

"Look, Lee . . ." He took her face in his hands. "What is this sudden comparison with Allison?"

She put her head down and he took his hands away. "I'm not comparing myself . . . Really, I'm not. I just wanted to know if I'm the kind of person that people could love."

"Any people? Or particular people?"

She didn't answer.

"Well," he said, *"I'm* a particular person and I love you very much. And so does Allison and so does Joel and so does your mother."

She sighed and kept her head down.

"Honey, nobody's loved by everyone she ever meets."

"I know that," Lee said, looking at him. "I don't want that. Then I'd be Mary Poppins!"

"And even *she's* not liked by everybody, namely *you* for one."

Lee laughed. "Okay, okay," she said. "I'm going inside to check out *TV Guide*."

"Fine."

Lee sauntered into the living room and flopped down on the couch. It was a small room and it reminded Lee of a motel office. The couch was one of those early American imitations, with flat maple arms, and cushions covered in a fabric print of barns, grange halls and lots of leafy trees. There was a coffee table in front of it made of the same yellowy maple, piled with program notes and continuity copy from her father's office. Lee dug *TV Guide* out from under the piles. The work from WNVL was the only thing in the room that was truly "her father." Even the pictures on the walls came with the apartment. He'd left everything either at the house for the new tenants or for her mother to take to New York. Lee thumbed absently through the magazine.

"Daddy! Guess what's on the tube tonight?"

"Wait, the water's running . . . Okay, what'd you say?"

"I said, guess what's on TV at nine? *The Desert Wolf!*"

"That's *The Desert* Fox."

"No, *Wolf!* It's a horror movie!"

"So was *The Desert Fox.* Hey, Lee, better come in here again. I need some help."

She sighed and put down the magazine. She loved the dishes her father cooked in the wok but hated to help in their preparation. There was too much cutting of vegetables and raw meat into small pieces with sharp knives and sharp knives made her nervous.

She leaned against the doorframe. Her father was deftly chopping celery into bits. Lee shuddered.

"How can you do that so quickly without cutting yourself?" she asked.

He smiled and kept chopping. "It's a talent, developed from years of watching horror movies with you. Listen, you don't have to use a knife. Mix a sauce for me, okay?"

"Okay. You're such a good cook, Daddy, someday you'll make some lucky person a good wife!"

"That is a chauvinistic remark, young lady . . ."

"You're right. I'm a throwback to another generation. What stuff should I use for the sauce?"

"Let's see . . ." He wiped his forehead with the back of his wrist. "Chicken broth, soy sauce . . . cornstarch in water."

Lee began to heat some water for the broth. "Well, how about *The Desert Wolf*? It looks good . . . A giant mutated wolf stalks this archeological dig and eats all the archeologists except one."

"Which one?"

"The one who catches it, silly. They have to keep one alive or there'd be no plot. How much cornstarch?"

He didn't answer. He was methodically dicing a chicken breast.

"Alan?"

He looked up and frowned. "If you're going to call me by my first name, then I will have to call you 'Miss Currie,' " he said.

"Sometimes it seems natural to me," she said, shrugging. "And anyway, it's 'Ms.' How much cornstarch?"

"A tablespoon," he said, ignoring her dig. "And a tablespoon of soy. A half cup of broth, but keep that separate."

The phone rang. "Get it, will you, Lee? My hands are wet."

She picked up the wall phone over the table. "Hello?"

"Lenore? Hi."

Lee wrinkled her nose. Allison was the only one who ever called her Lenore.

"Hi, Allison."

"Hi, Allie!" their father called from across the room.

"Daddy says 'hi,'" Lee repeated.

"Hi, Daddy!" Allison screamed in Lee's ear.

Lee rolled her eyes. "Allison says 'hi' back," she told him.

"I'm calling because Mom's not home and I have this big steak I defrosted this morning and it's too much for Joel and me and so what should I do?"

"Just a minute." Lee cupped her hand over the mouthpiece. "Allison says that Mother isn't home yet and what should she do with a big steak she's got for dinner?"

"Wait a second," their father said, reaching for a dish towel. "I'll take it." He crossed the room wiping his hands. "Allie? Hi, baby. You alone there with Joel?"

"Yes, we're fine, though. I just wanted to know— can I refreeze this steak or is it okay till tomorrow or what?"

"I'd cook it, Allie. If there's leftover meat you can make sandwiches out of it. Joel can take one to camp, right?"

"Uh-huh."

"So go ahead and cook it. Did the lamp for your room come?"

"Yes, this morning! It's nice, Daddy, thanks a lot."

"You're welcome, honey . . . Listen, baby, you're not nervous about being alone there?" he asked and began to twirl the telephone cord.

"No!" she said, sounding surprised. "'Course not."

"Well, okay . . . Put Joelly on so I can say hello."

Lee finished the sauce she was making while her father asked Joel about day camp and about his cold. She pushed the spoon down in the bowl to smooth out the cornstarch lumps.

"Oh, did she? Good. Put her on, will you, son?" her father said and Lee knew her mother must have come home. She mashed the lumps in her sauce as hard as she could.

"Hello, Elaine, how are things going?" His tone was flat. Purposefully flat.

"Not so well, yet, I'm afraid," she answered. "I've been to four job interviews in three days and I'm either overqualified or not qualified enough."

He began twirling the telephone cord again, twisting it into chunks of curls. "Well . . . That's an old story," he said. "At least you've gotten interviews, that's better than nothing . . . Look, Elaine, do you worry about leaving the kids alone there? In the apartment?"

"No," she said. "Why?"

"Well, because—"

"All last year while I was working they were alone, Alan."

"I know, but—"

"Allison's old enough and certainly more than able to take care of Joel and herself . . ."

"I *know*, Elaine, but it's New York City. *I* know New York and it scares *me!*" he said, louder.

"They are not wandering the streets, Alan!" she snapped back. "They are in a very safe, thick-walled apartment with a steel door!"

He knew she wasn't a fool, wasn't reckless, wouldn't endanger the kids for anything in the world. But they seemed so far away. Out of reach. It was true he hadn't seen the new apartment yet. He did want to know more about it.

"Well, is there a doorman?" he asked.

"No, no doorman. But a very effective buzzer system," she answered. "Now, look, I'm tired, I've had a discouraging day and tonight after dinner I've got to line shelves. I really don't want an inquisition right now."

"Elaine, I'm asking because I'm concerned about the kids. They're mine, too."

"I'm just as concerned as you are, Alan. Trust me, won't you?"

"All right. All right, Elaine. Listen, Lee's right here. I'm sure she wants to say 'hi.' "

Lee turned to her father. Her hand was tired from mixing and mashing. She hadn't realized the pressure she'd used.

Her father held the receiver out to her.

"Did she ask for me?" Lee said.

Her father bit the inside of his cheek.

"Did she ask to speak to me?"

"Come on. Just take the phone, will you, pal?"

Lee twisted the knots out of the cord. Then she said, "Hi, Mother."

"Honey, I'm sorry we haven't talked before this. I didn't want you to feel I was . . . on your back, as you always say. So I've tried to . . . let you get adjusted and leave you alone. I miss you."

Lee picked up a pencil and began to draw cubes on a paper towel. "Is your apartment nice?" she asked finally.

"Oh, yes . . . I hope you'll visit . . . see for yourself . . ."

"Uh-huh . . ."

"Are you anxious for your camp job to start? When is it, Monday?"

"Uh-huh. The twenty-ninth."

"Good. I'm kind of anxious for a job to start for me, too. My classes begin Monday, though, and I'm really looking forward to that! I have two . . ."

"That's good . . ."

"How are the girls? Virginia . . . Eileen . . . Connie . . . ?"

"They're all fine . . ."

"Well. Will you call me sometime?"

"Uh-huh."

"'Bye, honey . . ."

" 'Bye . . ."

Lee hung up and looked at the four cubes she had drawn. She crumpled the paper towel and threw it in the wastebasket near the sink.

Her father said, "Hey, now . . . Let's have that sauce you made so I can cook us a meal you'll never forget."

Lee smiled. "Until an hour later," she said.

Three

Long Beach was exactly what its name implied: a very long beach, broken up into several small sections with different names. Its sand was colored a mixture of beige and pure white with a stripe of dark tan near the edge where the ocean washed it. It was kept fairly clean by attendants, and on weekends, drew hundreds from the city.

Lee and her friends preferred Wrigley Beach, a remote section near the end, less frequented by beachgoers because of its distance from the parking lots. Lee and her friends didn't care about that; they could just chain their bikes to the entrance railing and walk right onto the sand. During the week, Wrigley was used by retired people and a few mothers with young children.

Virginia lay on her stomach in the sun. She was wearing her brand new, purple and pink bikini.

"Hey," she said, turning her head, "somebody un-hook my bra. I don't want a white strap mark across my back." The other three girls were lying on their backs next to her.

Lee was closest; she sat up and complied. "Don't worry, if anybody we know comes along, I'll hook it back in a hurry," she told Virginia.

"That depends," Virginia said, "on who comes along."

Connie groaned. *"Nobody's* going to come along," she said loudly. "There is no social life for the Shuffleboard Generation."

"The what?" Lee asked.

"The Shuffleboard Generation. That's Eileen's name. Tell her, Eileen," Connie said and nudged her.

Eileen said, "Mmmmph."

"She's sleeping. You tell me," Lee said.

"The Shuffleboard Generation," Connie explained, "means kids of split parents. Every other weekend they get shuffled off from one to the other. And sometimes plans are changed at the last minute between the parents so the kid can never make any plans. Y'know?"

"Mmm," Lee said thoughtfully. "I never heard you use that before."

"Well," Connie said, "you've been lucky so far. Both your parents lived within blocks of each other after they split. But you know how it's been with us every other weekend . . . Sometimes two in a row, sometimes not for a month . . ."

Lee rolled onto her stomach and began playing with the sand, letting it fall through her fingers and form a little pile.

"I'll be glad when camp starts," Virginia said. "I'm so bored." Her eyes were closed and her oiled face gleamed in the sun.

"Sure, Gin, you're going to love running around after little kids instead of lying on the beach," Connie said, grinning at her.

"Oh, you know what I mean. Maybe we'll meet some new people. *Male* people, that is. I have quite enough girlfriends, thank you. No offense, ladies. You'd think somebody would've had a party this week . . ."

"Why don't you have a party, Eileen?" Lee asked, still piling up sand slowly near the edge of the blanket. "Your mother's always out with Howard."

Eileen didn't answer.

"Hey, Eileen!" Virginia yelled, lifting her head. "Don't go to sleep on us, come on! You'll miss all the good gossip!"

"I wish we had some good gossip," Connie sniffed. She nudged Eileen again. "Wake up, Eileen, if you go to sleep you'll get a worse burn. Roll over or something."

"Mmmmm," Eileen mumbled. "What's the matter?"

"What's the matter with *you?*" Connie asked. "This is our vacation. We can't spend it sleeping!"

Eileen sat up. "I've got sand on me! It's sticking to my suntan oil . . ." She began to brush her arms off with her towel. "So what did you say about me behind my back?" She yawned. "Boy, am I tired . . ."

"Lee just said we should have a party at your house because your mother's always out with Howard," Virginia said.

"Not any more," Eileen replied. "They broke up last night."

"What?" Virginia sat up quickly and clutched at her bikini top. "Lee, hook me, quick." She turned around while Lee fumbled with the hook. "What do you mean, they broke up? Why didn't you tell us before? What happened?"

"Virginia, will you just shut up and let the girl talk?" Connie said. "What *happened,* Eileen?"

Eileen sighed and flopped over on the blanket. "That's why I'm so tired," she said in the middle of another yawn. "I was up with my mother all night. I'll tell you later. Let me sleep now."

"Oh, no, not unless you want more sand on you!" Virginia said, reaching for a handful. "Let's have the whole story."

Eileen opened her eyes. "I think you care more than I do, Ginny. Anyway, it's boring."

"I thought you liked Howard," Lee said.

"Just tell us who broke up with who," Virginia persisted. "Howard or your mother?"

"I'm still not sure," Eileen answered. "After sitting up talking to her all that time after he left I still don't know what happened. She kept saying it would never work out, so I thought *she* did it. But then she called Howard several very interesting names, so I thought *he* did it. Then she mentioned Artie, this guy at work—"

"Yeah, I've heard her talk about Artie," Virginia interrupted.

"So then I thought she was interested in Artie, you know, so she broke up with Howard over *that.* But then she started talking about this woman at *his* office, Howard's, so then I was sure it was over *that.* And then she said she was fooling herself all along trying to feel something for him when she really never did and all the time she wasted just seeing him alone . . ."

"So then what happened?" Connie said.

"She cried for about half an hour . . ."

"Howard did it," Virginia said firmly.

"Probably," Eileen mumbled.

"My mother says she doesn't trust any man," Virginia said, turning back onto her stomach. "That's why she has so many of them."

"Well, if I were my father, I wouldn't be so quick to trust a woman," Lee said.

"He hasn't started really dating yet, has he?" Eileen asked.

Lee shook her head. "No . . ." she answered.

"Oh, yeah? How do *you* know?" Virginia asked.

"He's been living in that apartment for six months now, hasn't he? You've only been with him a week or so . . ."

Lee frowned at her. "Well, I've seen him every weekend . . . And anyway, he'd tell me. We're very close."

"Mm-hmm," Virginia said. "Well, just wait till he does. And wait till he brings all his love problems home to you!"

"I wonder if men do that the way women do," Eileen said.

"I hope so," Virginia said. "I can't wait for Lee's dad to start, so we can find out."

"Do you think he'd like my mother, Lee? I know he's known her a long time . . . But I think he's sexy. Your father. I really do."

"Hey," Lee said, turning from one to the other. "It's only been six months!"

"Six months is a long time, sexually speaking," Virginia said wisely.

Connie grinned at her. "How do *you* know?"

Virginia smiled back. "Well . . . I don't. Yet. But my mother talks to me. And besides, it's been less than that since I broke up with my last boyfriend and I feel a definite lack."

"We know, we know," Connie laughed.

They fell silent. Lee picked up the plastic spoon she'd used with her yogurt lunch and began to dig at her sandpile. Virginia re-oiled her body. Connie dug out her reflector and tilted her face to the sun. Eileen stood up to brush off more sand.

"Lee, do you think he would?" Eileen asked, leaning over Connie.

"Would what?"

"Do you think your father would like my mother?"

Lee didn't look up. "I told you, Eileen, he hasn't even started dating," she said to the sandpile.

"Yet," Virginia said. "Hey, are there any cans of soda left?"

Connie reached into her beach bag. "Yup. But they're warm . . . Here, let me just shake it up for you . . ."

Virginia laughed. "Thanks, Connie, but no thanks," she said.

"Listen, Lee, if you don't think he'd like my mother just say so," Eileen said. "I don't like her much either!"

Friday at last. Alan Currie was washing his hands in the men's room at work, on the third floor of the WNVL offices. He was just reaching for a paper towel as the door swooshed open behind him.

"Alan, ol' buddy! How are ya?"

He closed his eyes and answered without turning around. "Fine, Stanley. How are you? Oh . . . swell!"

"What is it?"

"No towels. Our prosperous television station has

forgotten to replace the paper towels." He began rubbing his hands together over the sink.

"Well, kid, what do you want? We're not a big commercial station, y'know, in fact, we're not commercial at all, ha-ha!"

"I know that, Stanley, my job revolves around that fact, remember?" He took his handkerchief out of his pocket and finished wiping his hands. Stanley always called him "kid" and they were the same age.

"Listen, kid, I'm glad I ran into you, because have I got a chick for you!"

Alan Currie winced.

"No, listen," Stanley went on, "she's the best friend of this gorgeous lady I met at—"

He held up his hands. "Stanley, Stanley," he said quietly. "It's not that I don't appreciate all the efforts you've been making in my behalf since Elaine and I first separated, but—"

"Alan, you've gotta—"

"But I would really prefer to handle my own social life. Really. Okay?"

"You're making a big mistake, kid."

"Maybe, Stanley, maybe."

"Well, you're entitled to change your mind, you know. Drop down to Programming any time and let me know."

"I will, Stanley," he said and began to ease past him toward the door,

But Stanley was too quick for him. "Listen, kid,

you can't fool ol' Stan. I happened to be in Personnel when your new copywriter came in with her . . . forms. What's her name? Grace, uh . . ."

He turned back. "Stanley, look, the fact is, I've got my daughter Lee with me now. She'll be there all summer and that's a pretty full-time job—"

Now it was Stanley who held up his hands. "Okay, kid, okay. But that's some—new—writer in your department!"

"She's very bright, Stanley. She's had experience and excellent references!"

Stanley's laughter pursued him down the hall.

Grace Raphael, the new copywriter, was not at her desk as he walked by. Alan Currie was sorry.

Allison heard the key scratching in the lock that evening and ran to open the door for her mother.

"Hi, Mom," she said, taking a bag of groceries from her mother's arms. "How was it?"

Her mother sighed and stumbled into the apartment. "Fine," she said, "except it was not only full time, it was overtime, which means I'd have no time for my classes or for you kids—" she leaned over and kissed Allison's cheek, "—so it's not really so fine."

"So you didn't take it?"

"I couldn't. Honey, could you put the milk and fruit away for me?"

Allison looked in the bag. "I got milk and fruit today," she said.

Her mother tilted her head. "Oh," she said. "You did?"

"Uh-huh. And shampoo, too. We were running out. And I also got corn."

"Oh. Well, good."

"Mom," Allison said, starting for the kitchen, "you're tired and hot. Why don't you take a shower? There's cold roast beef and I'll make the corn, okay?"

Her mother smiled at her. "Sure. Okay. You're great, Allie," she said.

The cool shower felt good on her skin and she sat down at the dinner table in a white sleeveless wrap, enjoying the pampering as Allison served her.

"Mmmmm, this corn is good," she said.

"I boiled it too long," Allison answered.

"No, it's perfect. Isn't it, Joelly?"

Joel picked at his meat. "It's okay," he said with a shrug.

"It's all wrinkly," Allison frowned. "I'll get it right next time."

"When is Lee coming here?" Joel asked.

"Joelly, don't talk with your mouth full," Allison said.

"Lee's spending the summer with Daddy, Joel, you know that," his mother said.

"Why?"

"Because we all decided that would be best."

"*I* didn't decide," Joel said.

"Well . . . It was what Lee wanted to do. And your father and I agreed."

"It seems funny with everybody in different places," Joel mumbled.

"I know, honey, but you'll get used to it."

"Is Lee sleeping in my room?" Joel asked.

His mother sighed and put down her fork.

Allison glanced at her mother. "Hey, Joelly," she said softly, "Lee's in Daddy's apartment. The house is rented. You know that. You met the Perrys, the people who're renting it. You remember . . . Don't you?"

Joel looked at his plate. "You mean the family with two girls and a boy just like us?"

"Uh-huh."

"How come they all get to stay together in our house and we don't?"

"Joelly," his mother began, "didn't we all talk about this together? A lot of times?"

Joel didn't answer. "I bet the Perry boy is sleeping in my room, isn't he?" he asked. "Mom? Isn't he?"

His mother leaned over and put her arm around him. "Joelly, you have a brand new room of your own now. With all your things in it. And no one will sleep there except you, I promise." She kissed the top of his head. "Would it make you feel better if Lee came in for a visit? Would you like that, Joelly?"

"Is Lee coming?" Allison asked.

Their mother licked her lips. "Well, I was . . . thinking of asking her . . . I thought maybe over the Fourth. Next weekend. If she doesn't have plans . . ." She turned back to Joel and hugged him. "Wouldn't you like that, Joel? The four of us together again?"

Joel nodded and bit into his corn.

Asleep. At last. Both Allison's and Joel's doors were closed and there was no light visible from the cracks below.

Their mother put down the hammer and climbed off the stool she had been using in order to hang two small prints on the wall near the front door.

"Ow!" she said in a sharp whisper as her bare foot struck a tack on the floor. She picked up the tack and rubbed her foot, then stepped back to look at the pictures.

They were the only ones she'd brought with her. Two small details from a large frieze that they'd bought in Rome. It had been their first vacation since Lee was born, and there were still grandparents alive to watch the baby.

She shook her head to erase the memory. She had brought the prints with her because she'd always loved them, not for any sentimental reason.

She checked the floor for more tacks, then returned the hammer to the bottom of the linen closet where she kept her tools. No more hammering or noisy tasks now, with the children asleep. Now was the time for checking the evening paper for job listings. Of course, this was Friday, and Sunday's listings would be much better, she knew, but it wouldn't hurt to make sure.

She sat in the armchair, curling her feet under her, and picked up the paper and the red pen. She opened and folded the paper carefully. It was several minutes before she realized that all she had done was refold and crease the pages over and over again.

She put down the pen.

She knew she had no reason to feel sorry for herself. She was competent and capable and she knew she'd make it. Her classes would start Monday and the ones she had chosen were excellent, she knew she'd get a job . . .

It felt *good* to be alone. Something inside nagged that it was wrong to feel that way, but she felt it. Still, it was hard to be a single parent and this change, this move to the city, was hard, too. She felt no support from her family for any of the things she was trying to accomplish but when she thought about it, she really hadn't expected support. Certainly not from her ex-husband, and not from the kids, either.

She would rely on herself. If ever she let self-pity take hold of her, then she was through; the kids would know it and she wouldn't be worth a damn. She had what she wanted.

She looked over at the convertible couch in what

was supposed to be the dining alcove, but was now her bedroom. Each night it had to be opened up, each morning, closed. Not the ideal bedroom . . . But she'd had the ideal bedroom and it hadn't been the answer.

Four

The day camp was affiliated with the Long Beach Parks and Recreation Commission. Its facilities were located at the local elementary school, where Lee, Virginia, Eileen and Connie had all gone through sixth grade. Counselor jobs were hard to get and the girls had applied early for them. The hours were nine to two-thirty, and three times a week, a bus took the camp to the beach.

Lee was assigned to the youngest group, the six year olds. Virginia had second graders, seven year olds; Eileen, the ten year olds; and Connie, the oldest group, the twelve year olds.

The first day the four friends discovered that they'd hardly get to see each other. Even at the beach they were assigned specific places so that there would be close supervision of all the children.

At two-thirty, they all met at the bike-parking area and collapsed.

"I've had it," Eileen said. "We were better off at the beach."

Lee cried, "You! I'm the one with the six year olds! They can run around in ninety-degree heat and never even sweat, did you know that? It's a scientific law!"

"Oh, please," Eileen whimpered, "it's too hot to talk. Couldn't we just moan a little?"

"Come on," Connie offered. "Come to my house. The basement's air-conditioned. We can sit on the floor there and moan."

They sat on the cool tiled floor in Connie's finished basement, but only Eileen moaned. The others revived quickly in the air conditioning.

"Well," Virginia began, "I hope you all realize the summer's over."

"The summer's over," Lee repeated blankly, looking at Virginia as if she were a sunstroke victim. "The summer's over? Please, don't even kid about the summer being over—the words strike terror in my heart!"

"Well, it's true. You may think that that's not possible after only one day of camp, but it's not only possible, it's an absolute true honest fact," Virginia said.

"Don't ask her why," Eileen said from her prone position on the floor. She was stretched out so that as much bare skin as possible could touch the cold tiles. "I know why she says the summer's over. It's because she looked over the crop of boy counselors and discovered we know every one of them and they're all creeps."

"Do you believe it? There's not one new face in the crowd. They're all from Junior Junior!" The name of the school from which they had all just graduated was Martin Luther King, Jr., Junior High School. The tenth grade moved to "Junior Senior."

"Oh, come on," Lee said. "I saw Roger Peterson and Mike Semansky—they're both from Senior . . ."

"Oh, Peterson and Semansky!" Virginia cried, dismissing them. "They're both walking frogs' noses!"

Connie giggled. "Oh, Virginia, why don't you just run out into the street and scream 'I'm available!' "

Virginia sighed. "I would, but look what's walking around in the street. Well, at least I had a nice weekend. Yesterday, anyway. My dad took me to play tennis and then for Chinese food."

"My dad *cooks* Chinese food for me," Lee said. "And yesterday we went roller skating!"

"Your dad went roller skating with you?" Connie asked. "Gee, that's great, Lee. The outdoor place near the boardwalk or the indoor one?"

"The boardwalk one. And then we bought hot dogs and had supper on the beach." She leaned over and poked Eileen lightly in the ribs. "See, kiddo? I was the only date he had this weekend."

Eileen sat up. "Oh, Lee, your father's a man, isn't

he? He's going to be going out soon. You better not start getting hurt feelings over it or you're in trouble."

"Oh, I won't, I won't," Lee said. "I know he'll date."

"Never mind him," Virginia said. "Let's hope *you* do. And you and you and *me!*"

"But most especially—" Connie said, grinning widely.

"Me!" Virginia shrieked.

The next day, Lee went directly home from camp. She was tired and when the phone rang at five-thirty, it woke her up. She sat up dizzily on the couch, noticing that she'd left the television set on.

She turned it off on the way to the kitchen, yanked the receiver off the hook and grunted a hoarse hello.

"Hi, toots! How was your day?"

"Hot. Tiring. I was taking a nap. When are you coming home?" She looked at her watch. "Hey, it's after five-thirty. Isn't that your train time?"

"Yeah, that's why I'm calling. I won't be home for supper tonight. Okay? Can you manage?"

"Sure . . . I can go to Burger King or something."

"Have any money?"

"Oh. No."

"Well, there's some cash in my socks drawer. Under the box of slides for the 'Happy the Clown' show."

"Okay. You taking Joel and Allison out again?"

There was a pause at her father's end. "Uh . . . no. Not tonight."

"Oh. Who then?"

"Oh, someone from the office . . ."

Lee's eyes were wide open now. "A date? You have a date, Daddy?" She took a deep breath and let it out. "It's okay, you can tell me. I'm a big girl now and I've had a few myself."

He laughed. "Well, it's business, too. A new copy-writer in my department, Grace Raphael. We'll go through some scripts, discuss style, you know . . ."

"Mmmmm," she said. "*I* know."

"Sorry, Miss Worldly."

"Well, I am a few dates up on you," she said grandly.

"Only in this decade, sweetie," he shot back.

"Oh, boy, look out, Grace Redfield!"

"It's 'Raphael,' and knock that off. Listen, you'll really be okay? I promise I won't be late. Same time I usually get home when I take the kids out."

"I'll really be okay. Have a good time . . ."

"You, too!"

Lee hung up and dialed Eileen's number. Eileen's mother answered the phone.

"Hello, Mrs. Hillebrand," Lee said. "Is Eileen there?"

"Oh . . . It's you, Lee. How are you?"

"Fine . . ." Lee didn't ask how Eileen's mother was. She could hear in Mrs. Hillebrand's voice just how she was.

Eileen came on the line. "Hi. I can't talk too long. Since . . ." she lowered her voice to a whisper, *"the breakup,* I have to keep the line open. What a drag."

"You want to go out to eat with me? Burger King or something?" Lee asked.

"Oh, any other time, sure," Eileen answered. "But I feel guilty going out now. Especially at night—which is lucky, since I haven't had any offers. Anyway, how come you're going out? Are you alone?"

"Yeah."

"Daddy *out?"*

"Yes," Lee answered, annoyed.

"Now *that's* news! Look, how about coming over here for dinner? My mother certainly won't moan and groan with you around. It'll be good for her. And me, too! How about it?"

"Eileen . . . it's a business date. Appointment."

"I didn't even ask, did I?" Eileen said. "Come on over here, Lee, please? You need company and God knows we do!"

Lee changed her halter top and shorts for jeans and a tee shirt. She left the discarded clothes on the floor of her room, made sure to lock the apartment door and walked around to the back where she kept her bike.

She pedaled quickly and was soon out of the newly developed area of garden apartments. Eileen lived closer to Lee's old house in a neighborhood where there were large trees and sidewalks, instead of just grass, curbs and road.

Eileen's next-door neighbors had a porch with a swing and they were swinging on it as Lee rode up to her friend's front door. Usually she spoke to them whenever she saw them, but this evening she went right by to park her bike at the side of the house.

"That Lenore Currie's getting pretty stuck-up," the wife said. "Doesn't even say hello any more."

Lee stopped walking.

"Yeah, talking to the old folks is okay for little kids, but not when you get to be a young lady," the husband said.

Lee looked up toward their porch but all she could see were their backs.

"Hello . . ." she called. "Sorry—I was thinking about something . . . Didn't see you!"

They both turned around then and waved as Eileen stuck her head out of a window.

"Hurry up and get in here, Currie," she said sharply. "You're the first outside-the-family person to set foot in here for days!"

Eileen's mother made chili. Lee hated chili.

The three of them sat at the kitchen table but Eileen was the only one eating.

"You can at least try it, Lee," Eileen said, nudging her. "It'll burn out your kidneys."

Lee picked at it.

"You, too, Mom. You always love your own chili."

"I don't love it, Eileen, I make it because it's easy and cheap."

"Boy," Eileen snorted. "This is going to be a fun meal."

"At least we're all women," Eileen's mother said. "No men around to muck things up."

"Oh, come on, Mom—"

"I'm telling you girls it may sound like a cliché but men are all alike—mean and rotten!"

Eileen groaned. "Take a break from it, Mom," she said. "After all, we've got company."

"Now, Eileen, I've known Lenore Currie since she was practically a baby and if I can't give her and my own daughter the benefit of my experience, then I just don't know what!"

"Well, that's just *your* experience, okay?" Eileen said, but didn't wait for an answer. "Not everybody breaks up with Howard Millbank."

"It's not just Howard and it's not just your father. It's men. The minute you let them know how you feel they think they've got you right in their pockets and then they can just go do whatever they like. Just don't let a man know how you feel, that's all I'm saying, that way he'll stay interested. Wear your heart on your sleeve and that's when he goes. Bye-bye!"

Lee was looking from one to the other. She felt as if neither knew she was there.

She got up from the table. "My father isn't mean," she said softly. "Excuse me, I guess I don't feel very well."

"Oh, I'm sorry, Lee. I didn't mean anything about your father, really," Eileen's mother said. "Please sit down. I haven't been feeling so well myself lately and I'm just taking it out on you."

Lee sat. "And he's not falling in love, either." She looked over at Eileen. "He's not, Eileen, stop grinning!"

"Who's grinning!"

Later, Lee heard the phone ringing as she was turning the key in the lock. She opened the door quickly and raced for the kitchen. Her stomach knotted a little at the sound of her mother's voice.

"I'm sorry, honey," her mother said. "Where'd I get you from?"

"I was just coming home. From Eileen's," Lee answered.

"Oh. Your dad out?"

"Yes."

"Oh. Well, I called for two reasons. Guess what? I got a job today!"

"That's great, Mother! Congratulations."

"It's with a cosmetics firm, Je Suis Cosmetics, do you know it?"

Lee didn't, but she said, "Sure, uh-huh."

"Well, it worked out so well, because I can do most of the work on my own time, which means I'll be able to go to classes and get home to the kids and everything—" Her mother sounded breathless, genuinely excited. "It's mostly to do with marketing," she went on. "I'll conduct surveys and recommend new products and I get to hire people, you know, the ones who stand in Bloomingdale's and ask people to try new products—"

"It sounds nice, Mother," Lee said. Her mother hadn't sounded this happy in a long time.

"Yes, well, it doesn't pay all that much, but I'm just beginning and at least it's something I can contribute . . ."

Lee gathered that they were coming to the end of the job-talk. She suddenly felt afraid that her mother would ask where her father was, so she said quickly, "Uh, did you say you called for two reasons?"

"Oh. Yes. Yes, I did," her mother said. "I was going to ask you this anyway, but now it seems like sort of a celebration . . . I was hoping that maybe you'd . . . Well, you know this coming weekend is the Fourth of July and I was wondering, I mean, if you didn't have any plans, maybe you'd come in and spend the weekend with us. You know, there's so much to do, there are some nice exhibits at the museums or we could see a show . . . whatever you'd like . . ."

"Well . . ." A thousand thoughts raced through Lee's head at once. She didn't have any plans, but she didn't know what her father's were. She felt a surprising anger toward him which she couldn't acknowledge; whenever she'd felt angry before, her mother had always been there to receive it. Her mother had been a wall she might crash against. Still, a wall was a boundary. "I don't know what Daddy's going to do yet . . . Can I call you back?" she finally said. She wouldn't even suggest that her father might be out on a date. She didn't know how her mother would react and she didn't want to know.

"Sure, honey. Call me back. It's only Tuesday. Just tell me in enough time for us to make plans."

Lee hung up, but kept her hand on the receiver, not even realizing how hard she was clutching it. Something inside her was forcing her to put into concrete thoughts things she really preferred to keep fuzzy. Vaguely she'd decided that the summer would last forever and that her father wanted her as badly as she wanted to stay there with him.

But what if it were perfectly fine with her father that she eventually moved to New York? Was she cramping her father's style? Could he live a better life if she weren't around all the time?

Lee lifted her hand suddenly from the receiver and found that her fingers were stiff from holding it so tightly. As she flexed them, tears began to slide down her cheeks. Maybe she *should* spend the Fourth with her mother and the kids. At least she knew she was wanted there . . .

She sniffed loudly. Of course her father wanted her! It was silly to think he didn't.

Wasn't it?

As if to shut out all the thoughts, Lee raced to her room. She pulled out a loud rock album, put it on and turned up the stereo until nothing but a pounding beat filled her head.

Her father heard the music blaring before he opened the front door.

"Lee!"

No answer.

"Lee!" he yelled louder.

Instantly the music stopped. Lee came out of her room. "Hi," she said, leaning against the doorframe. "Have fun?"

"I did. Yeah," he said, smiling. "You?"

"Oh, yeah," she answered.

"Did you find the money?"

"Yeah, but I didn't need it. I went to Eileen's."

"Oh. Nice." He sank down onto the couch and patted the cushion next to him. "Come talk to your old dad," he said and yawned.

"Eileen's mother is down on men," Lee said, coming over to him. "She broke up with her boyfriend."

Her father sighed and rubbed his eyes.

"What's the girl like?" Lee asked. "The one you took out."

"Very nice. She's a copywriter, I think I told you. I explained to her the style we use at the station, you know, the tone we set with our station breaks—"

"And what kind of tone did you set with *her?*" Lee asked.

"Lee . . ."

"Well, I'm just curious, I mean, this is your first date, isn't it? Don't you think I'm entitled to know?"

He sat up straighter. "Wait a second, what's going on here? What did Gloria Hillebrand fill your head with, anyway—"

"It wasn't Mrs. Hillebrand!" Lee protested. "Honest. I'm just curious."

"Honey. It was only dinner. Nice lady. I'm entitled, right? I'm not in love. Okay?"

"Okay . . ."

"Hey. I'm sorry I snapped. I'll be asking you the same questions pretty soon, won't I?"

She smiled. "I guess so." They both leaned back on the couch. "Mother called before. She got a job."

"Did she? That's terrific! Doing what?"

Lee told him. "She wants me to visit this weekend. The Fourth."

"Oh, really? What'd you tell her?"

"I said I'd ask you what your plans were. What are they?"

"Me?"

"Because if you have a date or something . . ."

He turned to her. "Listen, Lee, don't let any plans I have interfere with what you want to do. You haven't seen your mother and the kids for a while and she might find some nice things for you to do in the city. It's okay with me. Really!"

Lee frowned.

Five

Lee watched the last of her campers being picked up at the gate. The little girl turned around and waved and Lee smiled and waved back. It was Friday, the end of their first week, and everyone around her seemed to look droopy and tired. Lee felt neither.

"What are you smiling at all by yourself here?"

Lee turned. It was Virginia, with a lock of damp hair hanging over her eye.

"Nothing, just waving goodbye to my kids." Lee began to walk toward the bikes.

"Hey!" Virginia said, "Wait! Where are you going?"

"Have to go to the store," Lee said over her shoulder.

"Well, you want company?" Virginia walked quickly to catch up. "What's your rush, anyway? There's Eileen . . . Eileen!"

Lee went straight to her bike and unchained it. She didn't want company now but she didn't know how to get out of having it. She wasn't in the mood for sharing her feelings with her friends.

She was going to spend the weekend in New York after all, and she had decided, at the last minute, to bring her mother a little present. A housewarming gift, maybe . . . Just a gesture . . . Something to start the weekend off pleasantly. She always managed to ruin things with her mother, maybe this would show she was trying . . .

But she didn't want to talk about it; whose business was it, anyway?

"Lee's going into town. Let's go with her," Virginia was saying to Eileen. "I want to get one of those big combs with the designs on it. I saw some nice ones at Rexall."

"Okay," Eileen said with a shrug and Lee sighed.

They all got on their bikes and rode out of the parking area.

"Come on, Lee, cheer up," Virginia said, pedaling next to her. "It's the weekend!"

"Fourth of July, whoop-de-do!" Eileen called from behind.

"Well, I'm celebrating!" Virginia cried happily. "I'm going camping!"

"We know, we know!" Eileen said. "You've mentioned it eight hundred times this week. Besides, I don't see what you're so happy about. Crawly things and freezing nights and burned food. Big deal. I went camping once. Never again!" Eileen pulled up so that they could ride three abreast.

Lee stopped trying to ride ahead of them and relaxed. She knew she would eventually tell them about her plans, it would just be sooner than she thought.

"How old were you?" Virginia smirked at Eileen. "When you went camping?"

"Eight, why?"

"Because I'm fifteen. And Mike is seventeen."

"Who's Mike?" Lee asked, joining the conversation.

"Her father's girlfriend's son," Eileen answered. "You know . . . Sandy's son."

"I didn't know there was a son," Lee said.

"Well, there is, and he's cute, too."

"You're going camping with your father and his girlfriend and her son?" Lee asked. "Like a double date?"

"Well, not exactly. Besides a son, there's also a daughter."

"Really? How old's the daughter?"

"Three. They had her to save the marriage."

"Ha! That always works," Eileen snorted as they braked their bikes. They were at the curb outside the drug store.

"Well, anyway, I know what you and cute Mike will be doing on your camping trip," Eileen said.

"Babysitting for little Save-the-Marriage while Daddy and Sandy start their own campfire."

"Oh, yeah, well, what will *you* be doing on the big Fourth, Miss Expert?" Virginia asked Eileen.

Lee thought, here it comes, they'll be asking me next.

"Listen," she said, "you guys go on into the drug store and get what you want. I'll meet you after I do . . . my thing."

"No, let's go together," Virginia said absently and then turned back to Eileen. "Well, what *are* you doing?" she asked as they walked into the drugstore.

Eileen sighed. "Staying here. I was supposed to be with my father, only my mother's so depressed I decided to stay home with her. Last year and the year before, she went up to Howard's place in Port Jervis. Now she's got nothing to do . . ."

"It's nice of you to stay with her," Lee said.

"Well, we were thinking of going to Port Jervis anyway and throwing firecrackers at the cabin."

Virginia bought the comb she wanted and began to browse through the cosmetics.

"I have to go," Lee said.

"Oh, okay . . ." Both girls followed Lee down the street and into the Card & Gift Shoppe.

"What are we doing in here?" Eileen asked.

"Have to get a present," Lee mumbled.

"Who for?" Virginia asked, suddenly sharp. "Listen, it may take me a while, but I do catch on, finally.

You're being very secretive, Lenore. Who's the gift for?" She looked at the glass flower Lee was examining.

"Not a man," Virginia said, turning to Eileen. "A glass flower is not a gift for a man. Eliminate father and secret boyfriend."

Eileen leaned in. "What are you doing this weekend, Lee?" she asked, and Lee couldn't help laughing.

"Boy, you'd make great cops," she said.

"Well?"

"Well what? You're so good at figuring things out. Figure it out!" She walked down an aisle and picked up a tiny ceramic fawn.

"You're going to your mother's this weekend, right?" Eileen asked.

"I thought you weren't going to be with her at all this summer," Virginia said.

Lee squirmed a little. There was another reason she hadn't wanted to talk to her friends: the cute sarcastic remarks that would be next on the menu. They'd be kidding, of course, they were her friends, but still . . .

"I know . . ." Eileen said with a leer. "Daddy wants to be alone this weekend, right?"

"No!" Frowning, Lee marched further down the aisle. I knew it, she thought. I knew they'd bring up something about that . . .

"Aw, come on, Lee." Virginia followed her and

sang playfully: "Shuffle, shuffle! Little sacrifices we children make for our parents, like leaving them alone for the weekend . . . I've done it a lot for *my* mom . . ."

"Hey, look," Lee said, facing them. "I'm going because I haven't seen my mother since she moved and there's a lot to do in New York and I haven't seen the new apartment yet and—" She stopped when she saw they were both grinning at her. "Well, it's true!"

Lee took the train to the city late the next afternoon, Saturday, the Fourth, under a cloud of discontent. Was she being shuffled? she wondered. Was her father glad she was leaving? What was he doing, anyway?

She thought everything around her seemed eerie. The Long Beach station platform was deserted; there were hardly any people on the train. It was eerie at Penn Station, too, and out on the street. Everyone in New York seemed to have left town for the big weekend.

She had no trouble getting a taxi. Her father had given her extra money for the fare but the meter kept changing so rapidly she wondered if she'd have enough. She took her wallet out of her little string bag and began to count the dollars and change. And what about a tip, she thought, biting her lower lip; you were supposed to tip, would there be enough?

She leaned back and looked out the window, still

clutching her wallet. This was the first time she'd ridden in a taxi alone. She'd been in one several times with one or the other of her parents; rarely did they take one as a family, there were too many of them . . . five people . . .

Well, she thought, not any more . . .

She began to think about her mother. She wanted this time to be a nice one . . . Would it be? Or would it be just another one of their constant confrontations? She caught a glimpse of her face in the taxi driver's mirror and noted its look of apprehension. She immediately rearranged it into a look of determination, then into a slightly forced smile. It was the best she could do.

When they arrived at her mother's building, she found that she had enough money. She tipped what she thought was generous until the cab driver glared at her before he drove away.

She stared up at the building. It wasn't large, just four stories. It looked new—white brick with a blue awning—but it was jammed in between some old and rather decaying brownstones.

She stepped inside the glass doors and located the small list of names with buttons next to them on the right-hand wall. Currie. 3B. Lee pushed the button and jumped as she heard her mother's voice over the intercom, "Is that you, Lee?"

"Yes, Mother." A sharp buzz sounded almost immediately.

She pushed through the second set of glass doors and faced the elevator.

Their apartment door was open and all three of them were standing there when Lee got off the elevator. Her mother rushed out to hug her. Allison came forward shyly and took Lee's suitcase. Joel stayed in the doorway and looked at Lee with wide eyes.

"Come on, I'll show you around," her mother was saying. "Of course it's not very big, but it is sunny. Oh, I'm glad to see you, honey, why'd you come in so late, it's after five . . ."

Lee had hardly said anything. She followed them all in and looked around.

"There are three bedrooms—mine, Allison's and Joel's. You'll sleep with Allison, she's got two beds in there, well, of course you know—it's her same furniture . . ."

Lee said, "Hi, Joelly," noticing that he hadn't said anything either.

"Hi," he said and gave her a tiny smile, which disappeared almost as quickly as it had come.

"He's been under the weather," their mother said with a slightly worried smile. "He keeps getting sore throats and colds . . ."

She reached out tentatively and touched Lee's face with her free hand. "I'm so glad you decided to come, Lee," she said. "I really am. Have you given any thought to what you'd like to do?" She began leading the way to Allison's bedroom.

"No . . . How's work?"

"I start officially, Tuesday. I'm really nervous, but thrilled, too. It's such a good beginning . . . Here we are." She put the suitcase down on the extra bed.

"It's small, isn't it?" Lee asked and then was sorry.

"Well . . . it's not a house, honey," her mother said, looking at her. "Anyway, if you only knew what apartments in this city cost! And actually, this is really a two-bedroom. My room is supposed to be a dining alcove. I've just blocked it off with a folding door . . ."

"It's nice," Lee said.

"Want to see my room, Lee?" Joel asked.

"Sure!"

"Are you going to live here?"

"Not now, Joel," Allison said. "I told you."

"We can't see a show," their mother said apologetically. "At least this time. It was too late to get tickets for anything and besides . . . I really didn't have the money. But there are so many other things to do . . ."

"It's okay," Lee said.

"I shopped this afternoon!" Allison interrupted. "And I got chicken and wild rice!"

"Look at my room, Lee," Joel said. "It's next to the bathroom."

"It's nice . . . the apartment," Lee said to her sister. They were alone in the kitchen. Allison had asked to fix dinner herself.

"Yeah, it's okay," Allison said. "How's your job at the day camp?"

"Not bad. It's really fun, but don't tell Eileen and Virginia I said that . . ." Lee smiled.

"Why?"

"It's more fun to complain. I have the littlest kids. They're cute. But there really aren't any boys. Y'know. How's summer school?"

Allison shrugged and leaned up against the sink. "It's all right. I have math, the one I flunked, and then I have this art class. That's just for fun. Still-life drawing and stuff." She began poking around in the refrigerator.

"So is that it?" Lee asked. "Two classes? And then what do you do? Go out with the kids afterwards?"

"Well, I don't really know anybody, yet, I've only been to classes once . . . But I have to pick up Joel at his bus stop at four, shop, clean up, get ready for supper . . . Hey, you want to make the salad?" She took a head of lettuce, two tomatoes and a cucumber from the refrigerator.

"I guess you'll have more to do when you get to know the kids," Lee said.

"Salad?" Allison repeated.

Lee frowned. "Why don't I do the rice?" she offered. "I hate knives."

"Oh, yeah," Allison said. "Okay, do the rice. Know how?"

Lee laughed. "No . . ."

"Okay, I'll show you . . ."

The phone rang and they both stopped.

"Mom still in the shower?"

"Guess so. I'll get it," Lee offered. "Hello?"

"Uh, Elaine?" A man's voice.

Lee stiffened a little. "No. This is her daughter."

"Oh! Allison! Hi!"

"This isn't Allison. It's Lenore."

There was a slight pause. "Who?"

Lee licked her lips. "Lenore Currie. Allison and Joel's older sister."

"Oh! Say, I'm sorry. Can't remember Elaine ever—"

"I'll bet you can't," Lee said and hung up.

Allison was watching. "Who was it, Lenore?"

Anger boiled up inside Lee. She began to feel hot and closed in, although the air conditioner in the living room managed to cool much of the apartment.

"Who was it?" Allison asked again. "How come you hung up?"

Lee glared at her sister. "Whose idea was it really for me to come in this weekend?" she asked.

Allison looked blank. "Mom's. Why?"

"I'll bet," Lee whispered.

"What do you mean?"

"Nothing. Just nothing. You better tell your mother to let her men know she's got three children," Lee said with a sneer. "I mean, I know it's out-of-sight, out-of-mind, but maybe you can jog her

memory about my existence every now and then!"
She raced from the room and down the hall.

Lee slammed the door of Allison's bedroom and leaned against it. The tears were already streaming from her eyes. She didn't even try to stop them but she made no sounds as she cried.

She wasn't sure which bed to flop on, which pillow to wet with her desolation.

It was true her mother had practically forgotten her. She hadn't really—*really*—believed it before, but now she knew it was true. Her mother never even thought to include Lee when she discussed her children with all the new people in her life . . .

Suddenly, Lee drew in her breath. Would her father do that? Would he mention her to the new people in *his* life? When he had that date last week . . . Did he talk about her, did he talk about his daughter?

The tears began again and Lee threw herself on the nearest bed, burying her face in the pillow. She felt very far away from Long Beach, very far from her father.

Her father at that moment was fixing his favorite dinner, chicken breasts with tarragon. He sautéed the chicken, then put it in the oven to keep warm.

He shaved with a blade instead of his electric razor, took a long shower, slathered himself with Brut and dressed: light slacks, open-necked plaid shirt with the sleeves partly rolled up.

Then he prepared the tarragon sauce, and tossed a salad.

Grace Raphael arrived on time but a little breathless. She had the use of her roommate's car for the whole weekend, and had taken a wrong turn driving out from the city. She apologized for looking frazzled.

He thought she looked wonderful. He thought they both looked wonderful. The martinis were perfect, the music he had chosen was perfect, the chicken was perfect or—he thought disgustedly—it would have been if they'd been able to finish it uninterrupted. But the telephone rang.

"I'm sorry to bother you, Alan . . ."

"What is it? Lee got there all right, didn't she? I mean, it's after ten, Elaine—"

"She got here, Alan, she's all right. Physically, that is. She won't come out of Allison's room."

"What?"

"She missed dinner. It's been almost three hours and she won't even answer my knock."

He sighed. "What happened?"

"Allison says someone called and didn't know who she was when she answered the phone, so she got insulted and just ran out. She asked Allison something about whose idea it was that she come visit this weekend."

"What? Will you run that back for me, Elaine? I don't understand—"

"I don't either, Alan, except someone called. I'm sure I know who it was, one of my partners on this case we're working on for my finance course. He thought Lee was Allison when she answered the phone, he didn't remember that I mentioned I had another daughter and why should he, for heaven's sake, we've just started classes and I barely know him, anyway that didn't seem to cut any ice with Lee. She apparently decided I didn't care enough about her to mention her to my friends, so—"

"Okay, okay, I think I get it." He glanced over at Grace Raphael, who had moved to the couch and was absorbed in a magazine. "And then she asked whose idea it was that she go to New York?"

"Apparently . . ."

He sighed again. "Maybe she thought I put you up to asking her?"

"I don't know what she thought, Alan. Maybe she thought *Allison* put me up to it. Or Joel! *Anybody,* if she thinks I'm neglectful of her . . . I don't know, Alan, honestly, I thought we'd straightened all that out, I really did—"

"Okay, okay . . . So she's been in Allison's room since the phone call?"

"Exactly. Well, it's her room, too. But I can't budge her. Neither can Allison. Even Joel tried—"

He smiled wanly at Grace who smiled back. "Look,

Elaine," he said, "what can I do from here? You've got to convince her that she's important to you, that's all. I can't do it. Talk to her, through the door if you have to."

There was a pause at the other end. Then she cleared her throat. "I shouldn't have bothered you," she said. "Of course you're right, I've got to handle this. Good night, Alan."

He and Grace managed to get through the vanilla ice cream with the crème de menthe sauce and almost all of their coffee before the phone rang again. He smacked his palm against the table.

Grace went into the kitchen for a glass of water as the phone rang on. "Listen, don't worry about it," she said over her shoulder. "I know how it is after a divorce."

"You do?"

"Sure. The man I just broke up with was divorced. He had twins. Eight years old."

"Oh . . ." He lurched toward the phone which would not stop ringing. "Hello!" he barked.

"Daddy?"

He sighed. "Yes, Lee."

"You took so long to answer . . . I was afraid you weren't home."

"I'm home."

"Yes," she said, sounding relieved. "I see."

"Are you out of your room, Lee?"

"I'm using Mother's phone to call you. They're all

in the kitchen. I want to come home. I'm coming home."

"Don't you dare, Lenore," her father said firmly.

"What?"

"Lee, you stay there. You haven't let your mother explain anything. Now that's not fair—"

"Oh. She called you."

"Of course she did. She was worried about you. Besides, under no circumstances are you going to get a train at this hour by yourself."

"Oh, yeah, she's so worried about me she doesn't even remember me when I'm not there!"

"Listen to me: You're being childish and unfair. Your mother remembers you and talks about you but she has no control over whether her damn *friends* who haven't even *met* you remember you or not! Now you get into the kitchen or wherever she is and you talk to her. And you listen to her!"

Lee didn't answer.

"All right?" he asked.

No answer.

"Lee, all right?"

"All *right!*"

"Don't be so tense, honey. It sounds like you were just looking for your mother to mess up. In your frame of mind she'll never do anything right."

"Goodbye, Daddy . . ."

"'Bye, Lee." He blew out his breath and hung up the phone.

"One thing about divorces," Grace said from her curled-up position on the couch, "you live half your life on the phone."

"I've noticed that."

"My ex-boyfriend? His twins live in Connecticut with their mother. He lives in New York. He begged the telephone company to install a special tie-line between their houses."

He rubbed his eyes. "I wasn't even thinking about the expense . . . Now that they're in New York, I'll have that, too."

"Divorce is expensive," Grace agreed, "in more ways than one."

He sat down next to her and smiled. "As of this minute," he said, "let's forget about divorces. Let's—"

The phone rang.

"I didn't take it off the hook," he said through clenched teeth. *"Why* didn't I take it off the hook?" He yanked the receiver from its cradle.

"Listen, Alan, she's gone. She just ran out of the apartment, I couldn't stop her. She came in here, we started talking and I don't know, it was just like it used to be, with neither of us hearing the other one, just yelling, and oh, Alan, I'm so worried about her out there by herself—"

"My God—I don't know what to do from here, Elaine. Couldn't you stop her *some*how?"

"Alan—"

"All right. All right. Do you have a train schedule there?"

"I've got one somewhere . . ."

"Never mind. I've got one. Hold on."

He raced for his briefcase in his bedroom, then picked up the phone there.

"Okay, they run every hour at this time which means—hey, how would she get to the station, anyway?"

"I don't know, Alan!" Her voice was frantic.

"All right," he said, trying to calm her and himself, "I'll just drive over to the station and wait for the train. I'll be here on this end. I'm sure she'll be okay. Elaine?"

"All right, Alan, just call me as soon as—"

"I will, I will."

He started to run to the door when he remembered Grace.

"I understand," she said once he'd explained hurriedly. "I understand." She tucked her purse under her arm and followed him out of the apartment. They got in their separate cars and went in opposite directions.

He didn't pass one car on the way and, gripping the steering wheel tightly with both hands, he got to the station in half the usual time. He pulled into a space directly in front of the middle of the platform, turned off the ignition, and flung himself against the backrest, pressing both hands against the ceiling of the car in a state of utter frustration.

It was a hot night. He undid the buttons on his shirt. He closed his eyes. I'm not supposed to be here, he thought. This was my vacation. No ex-wife, no daughter, not this weekend . . .

His eyes flew open. He realized he had pushed both of them out of his life as soon as Lee had gotten on the train that afternoon. Feeling guilty, he opened the car door, stepped out, and began to pace the deserted platform.

I wanted them out of my life, he thought. I did!! But wait a minute, wait a minute . . . It was only for the weekend . . . I didn't even ask for it, they *gave* it to me! This was *my* weekend, dammit, I don't ask for that much, I'm a responsible person, I love my kids . . .

He kicked at a telephone pole with the side of his foot.

One lousy weekend, is that so much to ask for? I have the right to be angry, don't I? They took away my weekend!

He sat down at the edge of the platform, resting his chin on his hand, feeling nine years old.

A train pulled in. He leaped to his feet, but the train didn't stop. It kept on going toward the next station, the last stop on the line. No Long Beach passenger on it, not even one.

He felt the panic, but calmed himself by breathing

deeply. He told himself that Lee would definitely be on the next train, for sure, the next one . . .

He got back into the car and turned on the radio.

Instinctively, Lee knew that it was safer to walk along a well-trafficked avenue than on a darkened side street. She was relieved to see as many people as she did, remembering the quiet streets of that afternoon.

Lugging her suitcase, she began to walk, then realized she really wasn't sure in which direction she'd find Penn Station. She was afraid to take another taxi—she might not have money for train fare if she did. And she had no idea where the buses went . . .

She began to feel slightly afraid. Not of the New York streets, but of her own impulsiveness in running away and what its consequences would be.

Her father had been right. Why should someone her mother just met, casually, in a business class, remember there was another daughter in the family? She *had* been venting her fears and anger on her mother, she *had* been looking to find fault. And her father loved her, of course; he was safe at home.

She stopped suddenly in the middle of the sidewalk, nearly causing an old man to bump into her. He muttered at her but she didn't hear, paid no attention, as she resolutely turned and headed back in the direction of her mother's apartment building.

Getting inside wasn't a problem. A young couple

with a large dog held the glass door open as she raced through.

She didn't wait for the elevator, but rushed up the stairs and only when she'd both knocked and rung the bell did she begin to be afraid of her reception.

"Oh! Lee! Oh, thank God!" her mother cried, pulling her over the threshhold as she embraced her. Lee could see she'd been crying. "Are you all right? Where did you go? I called your father, we've both been frantic—"

Lee could see Allison standing in the living room and smiled sheepishly at her. Allison smiled back, then looked at her shoes.

"I came back," Lee said, turning to her mother. "I was wrong, I guess."

"It was very dangerous . . . Going out that way . . . This isn't Long Beach, Lee . . ."

"I'm sorry," Lee said. "Look . . ." She pulled her suitcase over to the couch in the living room and opened it. She poked around inside and dug out a small package. "Here," she said, holding it out to her mother. "It's for you . . . I guess it's a housewarming present . . ."

Her mother took the package, wrapped in white tissue paper, and opened it tenderly and carefully, taking out the little ceramic fawn Lee had bought in the gift shop.

"I love it. I love it, Lee," she said softly. "What a nice thing to do."

Embarrassed, Lee looked over at Allison, who was still standing quietly in the same place. "Hi, Allie," she said. "Sorry I messed up your bed."

"It's okay, it was yours," Allison said.

"Joel asleep?"

"Uh-huh . . ."

Suddenly their mother clapped a hand over her mouth. "Your father!" she gasped. "We've got to call him right away!" She ran for the phone and dialed, tapping her foot as it rang.

"Let it ring," Lee said. "I know he's home, I talked to him before."

But her mother slammed down the receiver. "No. He's at the station, waiting for you. Waiting for your train."

"What train? What do you mean?"

"He thought you were on your way home. We both did. He's waiting at the station for you."

"Oh, no . . ." Lee sank down on the couch.

Her mother, just about to say "See what you've caused with this childishness?" looked at the tiny fawn she was still holding and didn't say it.

For the next hour they kept trying the Long Beach apartment. And then they finally went to bed.

"Mom? Mom!"

She awakened to the phone ringing and her daughter, Allison, standing over her.

From a dead sleep, she was instantly alert. She

knew without asking that Allison had been afraid to answer the phone herself at—she looked at her bedside clock—four-thirty in the morning.

"It's your father, Allie," she said reassuringly. "It has to be—"

As soon as she picked up the receiver she could hear him talking.

"—never came in. I've been going out of my mind—"

She felt dizzy from standing so suddenly. Scooping up the phone, she stumbled to the bed and sat on it heavily. "Alan, I'm sorry . . . We tried to call you as soon as Lee came back—"

"She's back? There?" His voice sounded tinny to her, faraway.

"Yes. Yes, she came back here. She's here, Alan, she's safe. I just wish we could have reached you—" She nodded and waved at Allison to go back to bed. Allison nodded back and padded out of the alcove. Lee and Joel had not awakened . . .

"Do you have any idea how crazy I've been? Every time a train pulled into the station I nearly got sick worrying she wouldn't be on it and when she wasn't . . . Dammit, Elaine, why couldn't you have handled this. Why is it that whenever you two are together it's like the bell rings and the referee shouts 'Shake hands and come out fighting!' It's always been like that with you and Lee and if you'd just made some attempt to understand what the kid was feeling and stop finding fault with everything she does, then maybe—"

"Now wait a minute! You want me to be the heavy in this, but I'm not about to stay there all by myself, Alan. No matter how justified you think you are!"

"Don't use that tone of voice on me! Don't make *me* into one of the children! Here I am trying to keep things on an even keel, holding things together—"

"You!" she retorted sharply. "You know, I didn't get divorced alone, Alan. *We* got divorced. *Both* of us. I'm tired of being made to feel it was all my doing, and that I'm to blame for everything."

"Stop it, Elaine! I'm telling you what I've been telling you for years—just give the kid some room. Get off her back. Just love her a little, can't you?"

She wouldn't answer that. "Listen," she said instead. "It's very late, and this isn't getting us anywhere."

"Wrong. It's getting me angry and tired. See if you can manage the rest of the weekend without me, huh?"

"Good night!" he heard her say.

He hung up and reheated the coffee. The birds in the garden stirred annoyingly. Right, Elaine, right, he thought. Maybe splitting was the best thing we ever did—except for the kids . . .

Six

He was waiting as Lee got off the train at the Long Beach station at seven-thirty Monday night.

"Hi Daddy," she said in a subdued voice as she slid into the front seat.

"Hi. Throw your bag in the back." He turned the key in the ignition.

She looked sidelong at him. "Sorry about Saturday night," she murmured.

He looked around the small platform. "I feel like I've lived here," he said. He backed the car out and began the short drive home.

"I'm really sorry."

"Let's not talk about it. How did the rest of the weekend go?"

"Okay."

"Just okay? Did you and your mother talk to each other?"

Lee sighed. "Yeah . . . We went to a museum yesterday . . . She talked about the pictures . . ."

"Mmm . . ." He glanced at her briefly.

"And she talked about her courses and about that new job she's starting . . . She kept trying to pull my hair back . . ."

"Did *you* talk about anything?" he asked.

Lee shrugged. "I don't know, I guess so." She peered out of the window, willing the car to get them home faster. Once her father swung into the parking space allotted to their apartment, she reached into the back of the car for her suitcase and almost ran for the door.

He followed, holding the keys.

As he opened the door, the noise from inside reminded him he'd left the television on and he cursed softly.

Lee laughed. "You're just like me," she told him. "A slob at heart!"

"Well, my room's neater," he called as she disappeared into hers. "Agh!"

"What's wrong?"

"They've got a news slide up and they're talking about an entertainment show!" he answered, glowering at the set.

"What?"

"It's the wrong promo!" he yelled.

"You're not supposed to watch NVL on your own time," she called.

"That's what you think!"

"Call the studio and tell them, then!"

"It's too late—" he stopped as the phone rang. "That's the studio calling me to apologize," he laughed and picked up the phone.

"Hi, Mr. Currie, is Lee there?" a voice asked breathlessly.

"Sure, just a sec." He covered the mouthpiece and yelled, "Lee!"

"For me? Who is it?"

"It's one of The Three, I guess," he answered.

She came out of her room and took the phone from him. "Hello?"

"Lee? Hi, it's me, guess what?" Virginia blurted.

"What?"

"Connie met a boy."

"She *did?* Where?"

"I don't know."

"Well, who is he?"

"I don't know that either. But Eileen called her when she got home from the movies with her mother tonight and Connie's mother said she was out on a date and Eileen said something brilliant like, 'Who with?' and her mother said some boy she met Saturday night and then Eileen called me."

"So nobody knows who she's out with?"

"Well, *I* don't and Eileen doesn't." Virginia paused. "Ooooh, I hate her!" she said finally.

"Oh, Gin, no you don't . . ."

"Yes, I do. Especially after the crummy weekend *I* spent."

Lee pulled out the phone cord and sat down on the kitchen stool against the wall. "No fun camping? What about Mike?"

Virginia snorted. "He didn't go. He had to be with *his* father. The plans got mixed up or something."

"Oh. So you ended up taking care of little Save-the-Marriage?"

"Don't even talk about it. How was your weekend in New York?"

"Don't even talk about it."

Virginia laughed. "All right. Then Connie's all we've got. Connie's date . . . He's got to have friends, right?"

"Unless he's weird . . ."

"Unless he's weird. So maybe Connie could have a party and he could bring his friends!"

Lee laughed. "Maybe. But first we ought to find out about him from Connie."

Virginia groaned. "But we can't do that until to-morrow!"

"Then let's hope we make it through the night."

"Let's hope!"

"You met him at the fireworks?" Lee asked, lean-ing on her bike the next morning before camp.

Connie nodded happily. "I was so bored Saturday night I decided to walk over there. I called you, Ei-leen, but there was no answer."

"I spent the whole Fourth of July weekend at the movies with my mother. Can you imagine anything worse? We were both so depressed we pigged out on chocolate almond bars." Eileen made a face. "I nearly went to the fireworks, but she didn't want to."

A bus full of campers pulled up to the school and cars began to arrive.

Virginia hopped up and down. "Come on, Connie, we've got to go to work in a minute. Tell us!"

"Okay. His name's Sam Cheney, he moved here three months ago, he's in eleventh grade, he's gorgeous, I'm in love with him and we're getting married."

"Boy," Eileen said, shaking her head. "That was some weekend!"

Connie laughed. "I'm kidding about the last part. Anyway, what happened was, he was on his way to get a hot dog over at one of the stands and he bumped into me in the dark and knocked me down."

"That's a cute way to meet," Lee said.

"Well, he started apologizing like crazy and then he asked if he could buy *me* a hot dog, which he did, and then he asked if we could sit together for the rest of the fireworks, which we did, and then he asked if he could walk me home, which he did. And we went out last night, too!"

"I can't stand it!" Virginia cried. "Listen, does he have any friends?"

"Boy, Gin, are you subtle," Lee said, poking her.

"Well, I would be, except we don't have time!" Virginia watched the campers skipping, running and strolling to their group meeting places. "Connie, here's 'subtle': I'm really glad you met someone you like. Now, that's enough small talk. Does he have any friends and how about having a party for them?"

"Come on," Lee said. "Let her think about it. We've got to go."

"I just met him . . ." Connie said hesitantly.

"You've been out with him twice," Virginia said.

"Well, I'll think about it," Connie said.

"See you at two-thirty!" Virginia cried and skipped off.

Eileen smiled. "Did you get the message, Connie? You're supposed to plan your party between now and two-thirty."

Connie rolled her eyes. "Yeah," she said. "I got the message."

When camp was over they bicycled back to the beach. They each carried bags with their bathing suits, still wet from the camp activity, but they were all wearing shorts and decided to wade in the surf.

Connie curled her toes deep into the wet sand. "Okay," she said, "who's where this weekend?"

"This weekend I'll be right here," Lee said firmly.

"Not me," Eileen said. "I'm finally going to be with my father for a change. Wouldn't you just know it'd be this weekend?"

"Oh, wait!" Connie said, kicking at the water. "I won't be here either! Well, friends, looks like that's it . . ."

"Why does it have to be a weekend?" Virginia asked. "Hell will freeze over before *we're* all together on a weekend! Let's make it during the week!"

"Yeah!"

"Where?"

"How about . . . my house?" Lee said, surprising herself.

"Really?" from Eileen.

"Why not? My dad wouldn't mind . . ."

"He has to get up early for work, doesn't he?" Eileen asked.

"Well, everybody does," Lee said. "It doesn't have to be a late party . . ."

"Great!" Virginia cried. "How about Thursday?"

Lee's father dropped his briefcase. "In this tiny *apartment*? On a *weeknight*?" he said. "I get up at six-thirty!"

"Oh, but Daddy, please? We can't do it on a weekend. All the girls get shuffled on the weekends."

He sighed. "Yeah, the Shuffleboard Generation, I remember. That's laying a guilt trip on your old dad, isn't it?"

"Yup."

"Hmmmm . . ."

"Anyway, it's only going to be eight people," Lee

said, bouncing around the room. "We can do eight people easy."

"Yes, but where do *I* hang out? I mean, what do I have to do, stay in my room all night?"

"You could go out," Lee said tentatively.

"Ohhhh, no."

"But it would be weird if you hung around . . ."

"Well . . ." he said, a thought crossing his mind, "what if I brought my own date?"

"What?"

"Why not? Why don't I have a friend of my own to talk to while you're partying around?"

"The new copywriter?" Lee asked.

"Why not?"

"No reason."

"Right."

"Right! No, you're right. I mean, we are two separate individuals with two separate lives . . . It's just that it's strange." She flopped down on the couch. "I can see myself being at a party but—" she barked a laugh, "I can't see you!"

"Thanks a lot!"

"No, really, I mean it's just so weird! Oh, Daddy, I'm sorry. I'll get used to it, I really will."

He sat down next to her. "I hope so," he said.

"Daddy?"

"Hm?"

"Do you really like this . . . new copywriter?"

"Yes. She's very nice."

"Do you think I'd like her?"

"She's not going to be your stepmother, honey."

"That's not what I meant. Besides, how do you know?"

He looked at her. Then away. "I—I just know, that's all. I mean, I've only been out of a marriage for half a year. I'm not ready to do that all again. So fast, I mean. Grace is nice, fun to be with . . . Look, if you meet a nice boy at your party, are you getting married?"

Lee shrugged. "Probably not. Except you never know, do you? You and Mom met when you were young."

"Right."

"Well, still . . . Anyway, you seem a lot better at this new dating stuff than I am." She peered up at him.

"I did go to a couple of parties. You know, while you were living with your mother at the house."

"Did you?" Her eyes grew wider.

"I didn't take anyone out after, but . . . I felt good. About myself. That I was a nice guy, you know?"

She giggled. "Of course, you're a nice guy."

"No, but I mean—to other people, besides just those who love me. We're both just beginning to have a kind of social life, only having the experience I've had, I probably look forward to it in a different way from the way you do."

She nodded. "I guess so. I'm scared. A little. Connie doesn't seem to be, neither does Virginia."

"Well . . . I bet they are."

"And you're not?"

He grinned. "Uh-uh."

"Why?"

"I was at your age, too, honey. You're just building confidence in yourself. As a young woman. I'm rebuilding mine as a man. An old man."

She laughed.

"And it's just not as hard as I expected it to be. I don't know why. It's kind of fun." He looked away from her. "Remember last weekend? Last Saturday night?"

She made a face. "Yeah," she mumbled.

"Well, I—I made dinner for her. For Grace. Here."

"You did?"

He nodded.

"You didn't tell me."

"Yes, I know. I'm telling you now, though. It's nothing to hide. Really, I don't know why I didn't tell you before."

Lee folded her arms and flopped against the backrest of the couch. "I guess I really knew you'd have a date last weekend . . . I just didn't picture it . . . here. How was it?"

"Well," he said with a smile, "I'd be able to give you a better picture if I hadn't had to leave in the middle to go wait for my daughter at the Long

Beach train station until about four in the morning."

Lee bit her lower lip. "Oh, Daddy . . . You should have told me!"

"Somehow, I didn't think that was the time."

"I'm sorry I wrecked it for you."

"It's okay. There'll be other times."

She turned to him. "Are you going to tell me all your love problems?"

"I hope I don't have any," he said. "But if there's ever anything you want to tell *me* for whatever reason, then you tell me. I want to hear it. Okay?"

"Okay. Does that mean for later, too?"

"Later?"

"When I—when I go to New York," she said and looked down.

He put his arm around her and pulled her close to him. "I like having you here," he said. "Before you came . . ."

"Before I came what?" she asked.

"It's hard to explain. I was married. I had three kids. Then suddenly, here I was in a silly garden apartment with nothing to show for it except a monthly cancelled check."

She looked up at him and he smiled.

"Now that you're here . . ." He didn't say any more but he hugged her again and stared at the wall. They had agreed. All of them. Lee would stay for the summer and join her mother, brother and sister for school in the fall. That was the plan. Everyone agreed . . . firm . . . He wanted to be fair. And suppose there was the possibility of Lee staying with him. She'd be choosing, in effect. Taking sides. He couldn't put her in that position . . .

And what about his own life? Was he ready to commit to being a full-time single parent? Sure, the summer was great, but there was a deadline on that . . .

With his arm still around her shoulder, he looked at her face. His daughter. His pretty daughter. His first child . . .

His throat tightened.

In New York City, Allison came into the living room holding her drawing pad. Her mother looked up from her prone position on the couch. She had begun her new job that morning, and though she had really just "gotten her feet wet," as she said, she felt exhausted.

"Allie? Is that your art work? May I see it?"

"Okay . . ."

Allison brought the pad over and her mother sat up.

"Nice!" she said, turning pages.

"Not really. You should see some of the other students' . . ."

"Oh, come on, Allison, this is good of the flowers . . ."

Allison dismissed that with a wave of her hand.

"You always loved to draw," her mother said. "Don't you like the class?"

"It's better than math," Allison answered.

"Well," her mother said, looking around, "I must say this living room is a work of art. It looks absolutely spotless. I was noticing it while I was lying here."

Allison smiled for the first time. "I polished the floor and I waxed the chairs and those shelves on the wall."

Her mother shook her head. "I'll say you did. When did you have time for all that?"

"Oh, while Joel was in camp. Before classes."

"And after classes?"

"I brought Joel home and finished."

Her mother frowned. "Allison, sit down," she said and patted the cushion on the couch. When Allison complied, she took the girl's chin in her hand. "You know," her mother began, "I'm very proud of the way you seem to have taken over here . . . But I'd really love to see you find some fun things to do while Joel's in camp . . . There must be some nice kids in your classes . . ."

"Are there nice kids in your classes?" Allison asked, pulling away.

"What?"

"I just meant . . ." she shrugged. "You go to school too, and work, but you come home right after . . ."

"Oh, Allie, that's different, I'm not twelve years old."

"Well, what about that man who called here?"

"What about him?"

"I don't know. I was asking you."

Her mother smiled. "He's twenty-five years old. We're working on a case together. The professor assigns us cases, about particular businesses, and we analyze them and prepare ourselves for questions from the class." She waited for Allison to comment, but Allison just looked at her. "See?" she asked finally.

"I see . . ."

"But that doesn't answer my question about you. You seem to be spending more and more time around the house . . . Cleaning, cooking, shopping, babysitting . . . Those are all very grown-up tasks and while they're appreciated, I really wish you'd—"

"Did you know Lee's having a party?" Allison said quickly.

Her mother drew back. "Is she? How do you know?"

"I talked to her on the phone when Daddy called us. She told me."

"Oh. When?"

"Thursday, I think . . ."

"During the week?" She frowned.

"I guess . . ."

"Oh . . ."

Allison stood up. "I'll be in my room," she said, but her mother didn't answer.

She went into the kitchen, picked up the phone and dialed. He answered.

"Alan? Hello. It's me."

"Hello, Elaine."

"I understand Lee's having a party . . ."

"Uh, yes, as a matter of fact . . ."

"And it's on a weeknight?"

"Yes, Thursday. Why?"

"Will you be there, Alan? I mean, you will chaperone—"

"Yes, Elaine, I'll be here."

She imagined the exasperated expression on his face. "Well, um . . . Do you know what to serve? How many people are you having? Will there—"

"Listen, Elaine, why don't I put Lee on for this, okay? She can answer for herself . . . Lee!"

After a moment, she heard her daughter's voice: "Hello?"

"Hi, honey. I hear you're having a party."

"Yeah . . ."

"This is the first one you've ever had!"

"I guess—"

"I mean, since you were about ten . . ." She laughed a little. "Do you know what you're going to serve?"

"Um—"

"Have you planned it? How many are you having?"

"Eight—"

"Because if you need to buy anything—"

"Listen, Mother—"

"What about drinks? You'll have just soft drinks, right? Does anyone drink beer? Do you know everyone who'll be there?"

"It'll be fine, Mother. Don't worry about anything. Please."

Her mother sighed. "I didn't mean to be pushy, Lee. Honestly I didn't. I just wanted to help. Your first party . . ."

"It's okay. Thanks."

"I hope you have a good time." She bit the knuckle on her finger. Everything she said to Lee seemed to aggravate her.

"Thank you."

"If there's anything I can do, just call. Those little frankfurters wrapped in dough are always—"

"I will. I'll call," Lee said.

Seven

Grace Raphael came for dinner before the party. She wore jeans and a light blue puffy-sleeved cotton sweater.

Lee's father adored his daughter for not making one wisecrack, and for her efforts to be polite and sweet to Grace. He felt himself smiling all the while they ate. The phone didn't ring once and the iced shrimp was superb. An excellent omen for the evening ahead.

Lee didn't smile much. She thought Grace Raphael had the sense of humor of a wet sneaker, no match for her father's at all. To avoid being engaged in conversation, she leaped up throughout the meal to clear the table and serve new dishes. The phone was quiet the entire time and the mayonnaise was green. An evil omen for the evening ahead.

The girls arrived first, in a clump. Lee introduced them to Grace and as she watched their faces she almost wanted to laugh. Quickly she swept them into her room and closed the door.

"Now look," she said, "before you say anything, they only just met. Besides, she's a dog."

"She doesn't look like a dog," Eileen noted.

"You know what she said at dinner tonight?" Lee said, curling her lip. "She said I'd look so pretty if I'd just pull my hair back off my face, like *this!*"

"Sounds like your mother," Connie said.

Lee said, "*Tell* me."

"Does your father seem a lot different?" Virginia asked.

"What do you mean, different?"

"Well, what was he *like* with her? At dinner, for example. Was he trying to impress her every minute?"

"Oh, stop it Virginia," Lee said, turning away.

"Listen, don't be touchy, Lee. He's supposed to do that. It has been a while, hasn't it? You should have seen *my* father when he was first going with Sandy. The phone would ring, I'd yell, 'It's Sandy!' and he'd get all goopy and runny, like a head cold."

"What about now?" Eileen asked. "He's been seeing her over a year."

"Oh, now it's fine. It's like they're married, except they have more sex since they don't live together."

"Well," Eileen said with a grin, "I think it's kind of cute, Lee. You and your daddy having your first dates at the same time. A double debut!"

Lee threw a panda bear at her.

The boys were late. All four arrived at 8:35. Lee could hear them talking and laughing loudly outside the door until one of them rang the doorbell. Then there was a deathly silence.

Connie was the only one with a specific date. No one else was to be paired off. It was expected that the other six would mix, mingle, and eventually zero in.

"Uh, this's Warren, this's Ivan, this's Buff," Sam Cheney mumbled, indicating each with a wave of his hand.

The girls said, "Hi. Hi. Hi," glancing briefly at them and back at each other.

"Connie told us you just moved here about three months ago," Virginia said to Sam. Virginia talked easily to boys.

Sam said, "Yeah, that's right. From New Jersey. My father decided to come back to the family business and work with his brother."

The three girls said, "Oh," and the conversation stopped.

"It's a printing firm," Sam said finally.

Everyone nodded.

Lee was terrified by the silence. "Why don't we sit down," she said, tilting her head toward the living room couch and chairs. "It'd be more comfortable, would you like something to drink, how about some music?"

No one answered the questions but they all sat down; Eileen and Virginia in separate chairs, Lee and the boy named Warren on the floor and Connie, Sam, Ivan and Buff on the couch.

"Where'd you get the name Buff?" Eileen asked, looking at Ivan.

"He's Buff," Ivan grinned.

"Oh, sorry." Eileen turned red.

"I was named for my father and to avoid the confusion, they just gave me the nickname," Buff said.

"Oh, it's a nice name," Eileen said quickly. "What's your real name?"

Buff smiled and rubbed his finger along the edge of the couch. "Oh, ask me later when I know you better," he said and now his face was red, too. Eileen poked Virginia. She liked him.

They played records and danced a little. They all drank soda and ate pretzels and peanuts and later, pizza, which the adults went to pick up. Connie and Sam sat together and talked most of the evening. Sam had his arm around Connie. Lee and Warren, finding themselves on the same side of the coffee table as they sat on the floor, began a halting conversation. Virginia was stuck with Ivan who she decided was boring.

"You lived in California?" Lee asked Warren softly, her eyes widening.

"Up till last September. I was born there."

"I've never been that far west," Lee said. "It's always been 'one of those far-off places' to me. Do you miss it?"

"Well . . . sometimes. I had a lot of friends there. But," he smiled at her, "I like making new ones."

"Did you go surfing?"

"Some."

"You can do it here. At the beach."

"I know. I don't get much chance, though. I've got a job."

"Me, too. At the day camp. What're you doing?"

"Well, I'm really interested in photography. I'm working at the Carroll Studios, you know, building sets, mixing chemicals, taking exposure readings, learning the business . . . I like portrait photography a lot."

"Sounds nice. I mean, to be able to work at something you really want to use later on . . ."

"Today, a woman brought her cat in for a portrait."

"Really? Her cat?"

"Oh, yeah, we do a lot of animals. But this cat refused to sit on the pillow she brought. He kept arching his back and hissing at all of us."

"What did you do?"

"Oh, Mr. Carroll got some great shots of that, but the woman didn't want those. She wanted her little cat happy and smiling. We finally got it, though. You have to know how to calm them down."

Lee looked at his hands for the first time and saw they were covered with tiny scratches.

"I see you know how," she smiled.

Warren laughed. "Babies are funny to take pictures of. You find yourself doing the weirdest things to get their attention!"

"Oh, I'd love to watch that," Lee said, clapping her hands together, and then looked down shyly. "I mean, it must be fun."

Warren looked at her for a moment. "I'd like to show you sometime. You know, how we take babies' pictures . . ."

Neither of them spoke for a moment. Then Warren said, "You know . . . I think I'd really like to photograph *you* sometime . . ."

"*Me?*"

"Yeah . . . I was just watching you while you were looking down there—no, there. With your face just slightly turned—" He touched her cheek and moved her head just a little. "Like that. Yeah, that'd be a nice shot. A study. Without a smile or anything." He kept his fingers on her cheek.

Lee felt herself color slightly. She was afraid to move in case he took his hand away. Then he reddened, too, and pulled his hand back.

"You, uh, you like your job?" he asked finally.

"I'm lucky to get it," she answered. "There aren't many jobs open for kids our age. You're lucky, too. You've been here such a short time and you not only have a job, but one you really like."

"Yes, but I hounded Mr. Carroll. I've been haunting his shop since way before school let out. Even

working for free and stuff. For the privilege of using—"

Warren began to describe some of the equipment
he was allowed to handle. Lee watched him as he
talked. She hoped he'd touch her again.

"I guess," he said finally, "that I should have spent
a little more time around school. Then maybe I'd've
met you sooner."

Lee's heart gave a little jump.

"I guess your folks are divorced," he said.

"Just recently . . . But they separated in January."

"Yeah. Seems to be an epidemic."

"Why?" Lee asked. "Are yours?"

"Oh, no, but at least half the people here—" he
swept his arm around the room.

"I guess that's true," she agreed. "It won't happen
to me when I get married."

"Oh, me neither," Warren said. "I really believe in
permanent relationships. I was beginning to have
one in California, but then we moved. You can't
keep anything up when you're that far away from
each other."

Lee's heart sank. She hated some unknown girl in
California.

"But it was only just beginning, so the attachment
wasn't that deep, you know?"

She didn't know. Her attachment was deep and it
was only ten-thirty.

"Anyway, it's really over," he said. "We're not even writing."

Lee sighed.

"I really would like to photograph you some time," Warren said, studying her again. "I bet with your hair back—" He reached over and pulled a heavy hank of waves away from Lee's face. "Oh, see? You have such pretty cheekbones, you can really see them now."

Connie, who looked up to see Warren holding Lee's hair back, involuntarily giggled to herself.

The adults enjoyed their pizza and beer in the kitchen.

"This is fun for me," Grace said, smiling.

"I'll bet."

"No, really. It reminds me of my first party. It looks like Lee hit it off with one of the boys."

He looked at Lee with Warren and nodded slowly.

Grace added, "I wish she'd liked me, but I guess I didn't stand a chance."

"Of course she liked you, what do you mean?" he asked indignantly.

Grace shook her head. "No, Alan. But it's not me. It would be anyone you took out first."

He rubbed his thumbnail over his lips and frowned.

Grace pushed the last of her pizza crust into her mouth and wiped her fingers. "Everybody I know who dates a divorced man has trouble with his kids, especially in the beginning. Probably because the man doesn't really know where he's at, either, and the kids get nervous. You know—everything's changing for them."

"Mmmmmm," he said thoughtfully, and Grace repeated, "Mmmmmm," and smiled at him again.

Warren was the last to leave the party. Eileen, who was supposed to sleep over, decided to go home, since Buff had asked to walk her there. She had left all her overnight things in Lee's room, not wanting Buff to know of her original plans. Virginia had been the first to leave, Ivan a close second. Lee didn't even remember when Connie and Sam left.

What she did remember was Warren's leaning down to kiss her good night; Warren's telling her that she was the best thing that had happened to him since he left California; Warren's saying that he liked to watch her face while she was listening to him, or listening to music, or listening to anything.

Warren Fish.

Warren Fish.

Lee wrote the name all over her desk blotter. She went to her mirror and pulled her hair off her face. She began to braid it the way Eileen sometimes did, with one braid hanging down her back. She decided she really did have beautiful cheekbones, she just never noticed them before.

She decided that Warren must be a great photographer, a truly sensitive photographer. He liked portraits, maybe he'd like landscapes. Maybe they could take their bikes somewhere near woods or streams, or maybe they could go to the beach and he could photograph her there. At the beach. She had to get a new bathing suit!

Lee flopped onto her bed. But she couldn't sleep. She knew that her father was driving Grace into the city and it didn't bother her. She felt good.

A boy really liked her and showed it. Not like the silly kids she had flirted with since fifth grade. This was different. A boy she could really talk to, not just throw meaningless words at. A boy she could talk with about her real inner feelings, as she could with her close girlfriends, only better . . . This was new, this was different. She'd never really talked with a boy before. *Really* talked.

Her father knocked on her door then. She sat up, jumped off the bed and hugged him.

"Good party?" he asked, holding her slightly away in order to look at her face.

"Uh-*huh!* Did you like him, Daddy?"

Her father smiled sheepishly. "I guess . . . I didn't really meet him, honey. What's his name, anyway?"

"Oh, Daddy . . . Warren! Warren Fish. He's a photographer."

Her father frowned. "He doesn't go to school?"

"Sure he goes to school. But now he's working as a photographer. Well, a photographer's assistant. That's what he wants to be. He's really cute, isn't he?"

"Really cute," he answered. "Get some sleep. You'll never make it through camp tomorrow."

Alone in the living room, he snapped on the television, tuned to WNVL and flopped into a chair. He thought about what Grace had said about trouble with divorced men's kids. Lee *had* seemed anxious before, but she was far from anxious now. She hadn't even mentioned Grace and here he'd just driven her back to New York. All Lee'd talked about was Warren . . .

Maybe now that Lee's got this new romance, he thought, there really wouldn't be problems with his own dating. Well . . . He looked up at the test pattern on the TV screen. He hadn't even realized it was so late WNVL had signed off.

Eight

Warren didn't finish work until five. Each day at two minutes after, he and Lee met outside the studio. They usually had an hour and a half to be together until Lee's father got home and Warren's family had dinner. They spent most of the time talking. And walking. Warren took pictures of Lee in front of the studio, sitting in a garden, hugging a tree trunk, standing on a fence, reading a book, laughing, thinking, or generally radiating her feeling for him.

She loved posing for him. She felt she understood at last what all the talk about being a woman really meant. She felt alive for the first time. All the things that used to be so important suddenly weren't.

Lee thought she was the luckiest girl in the world. Warren Fish adored her and Warren Fish was gorgeous and brilliant and funny and sensitive and talented and wise. Every day brought new insights and discoveries and Lee floated through each one.

Her father observed her frantic social schedule with mixed feelings. He felt he was watching himself slide over on the bench to make room for the new all-important man in his daughter's life.

July sped by. Lee was radiant and her father relaxed. Both their days and evenings were fuller. He felt safe in calling up at the last minute to say he'd be home late; Lee rarely asked, with real interest, whether he'd be with Allison and Joel or whether he'd be on a date.

He knew Lee would be all right. She didn't take advantage of the freedom he gave her. She was never out too late during the week, though he had the feeling that was due more to Warren's concern about his work than Lee's about hers. On weekends, she was usually home before he was. Sometimes Warren was there and he'd find them in the kitchen having a snack or in the living room watching TV.

Warren always leaped to his feet to shake his hand, unnerving him a little, but still pleasing. And the way Lee looked at that boy made her father almost wish he were a teen-ager again.

But not quite . . . They're so intense, he thought . . .

A Saturday night.
"Going out tonight, honey?"
"Uh-huh. You?"

"Yes, matter of fact . . ."

"With Grace?"

"Grace? Well, no . . ."

"*No?*"

"Not tonight . . . This is a nice woman I met while I was over at the studio. She's with the network."

"Ohh! No more Grace?"

"Oh, sure. I see Grace. How about you? Are you going out with Warren?"

Lee pulled a face. "Of *course,* Daddy. I'm not fickle."

"Hmmm. Where are you going?"

"To a party. With Eileen and Buff. Do you like this top? Warren says lavender is my best color."

"Terrific," he mumbled. *I'm not fickle,* he mimicked in his head. He turned his face away. He couldn't bear to watch his little girl putting on lavender eye shadow to match her shirt. He wondered if in a few years his daughters would only remember him as "that man who lived with our mother when we were little."

He shook his head to clear it. He knew he was being silly.

"Warren's right, it's your best color," he said and smiled at her.

"One morning in early August, his secretary buzzed him. "Your wife's on three, Alan," she said.

The words sounded strange to him. His wife. Now he didn't think of himself as having a wife.

He pushed the third button on the phone. "Elaine. What's up?" he said brusquely.

"Hello, Elaine, how are you? Fine, thank you," she said.

"Sorry."

"I'm sorry to disturb you at work, Alan, but I can never get you at home in the evenings any more."

"Well, you know when I'm with the kids . . ."

"I know when you're with Allison and Joel. I don't know when you're with Lee. Are you leaving her alone a lot, Alan?"

"Lee is just fine. She's a big girl, she's got friends of her own she wants to be with."

"She won't even talk about coming to visit here again . . ."

"Well, she's got a boyfriend now. You know how that is, Elaine . . ."

"I know she needs some supervision, too, Alan . . ."

"Look. I really don't want to get into this right now. I'll call you back. Tonight. Okay?"

"Wait . . . Alan . . . I didn't call about that. I called because Joel has to have his tonsils out. Adenoids, too, probably. I mean . . . I knew you'd want to know."

"You're right, Elaine. Thank you . . . When?"

"Well, he's got another cold right now, so when

he's over it, I guess. This month, though, so he'll be fine when school starts."

"Just let me know when, I want to be there," he said.

"Hi, Lee! Where's your group?" Eileen was watching her ten year olds on the volleyball court.

"I left them with Kara. I have to ask you something." She sat down on the grass next to Eileen. "Are things the same with you and Buff?"

"The same?"

"I mean, is everything . . . okay?"

"Sure."

"Do you like him as much as you did in the beginning?"

Eileen turned toward her. "I guess so. Why, don't you? Like Warren the same?"

"Yes. But something's different about *him.*"

"What?"

"I don't know, that's just it. Something is, though. Like . . . every day we'd meet at five at Carroll's?"

"Yeah . . ."

"Well, he told me not to come today. He said he had to go right home."

Eileen caught the volleyball that would have otherwise bounced off Lee's head and threw it back to her girls. "So?" she asked. "He has to go right home. So what?"

"Last month he would have told me to meet him

anyway just to be together. And maybe I'd walk him home."

Eileen frowned. "Lee, you're getting paranoid."

"You think so?"

Eileen nodded. "I mean, unless you had a fight or something . . ."

"No. We didn't have a fight. That's just it. But . . ." She stopped suddenly and turned away from Eileen.

"But what? Come on, say it."

"You don't have to fight to break up. People get bored with each other without fighting. Like my mother . . ."

Eileen made a face. "Lee, your parents fought plenty, I remember you talking about it all last year. There were lots of fights. Your mother didn't just get bored."

Lee nodded. "Well, Warren and I haven't fought at all. And I haven't changed. So if he liked me a lot once, he can like me a lot again. I can make him like me again!"

That night, Lee waited for Warren to call. She was sure he would; they hadn't seen each other all day. She lay on her bed and made up counting games: Warren would call before she reached 100. Then 125. Finally, 500.

He didn't call. Her father was out. She wasn't sure with whom, but Lee didn't know if she could talk to him anyway. She tried to tell herself she was being paranoid, as Eileen said. But she couldn't shake her creepy feelings and her stomach ache. She couldn't even cry.

When her father came home later she was sitting in front of the television set in her nightgown.

"Hi," he said cheerfully. "Shouldn't you be in bed? You've got work tomorrow."

"So do you," she said without looking up. "Were you in bed?"

"Hey!"

"I'm just kidding, Daddy . . ." But she didn't smile and she still didn't look at him. "Did you have a good time?"

"It wasn't a date. I told you. It was a planning meeting."

"Oh. I forgot."

"What's so absorbing?" he asked, sitting down next to her. "Good movie?"

"I don't know . . . I wasn't paying attention. Allison called . . ."

"Aw . . . sorry I missed her. Too late now, I'll have to call her tomorrow . . ."

"She was hysterical."

He sat up straight. "Why?"

"Joel has to have his tonsils out."

"I know. Your mother told me. Why was Allie hysterical?"

Lee curled up on the couch so that her chin rested

on her knees. "She was worried. She acted like he was going in for open-heart surgery or something."

Her father ducked his head to try to read her face. "Aren't you worried?" he asked.

"Oh, sure, but people don't die from getting their tonsils out. I mean, he'll be home the next day, won't he?"

"Sure . . . Say, what's the matter with you, anyway?"

"Nothing . . . Mother wanted me to come in this weekend . . ."

"Uh-huh?"

"But I said no."

"Seeing Warren, huh?" he asked.

Lee uncurled her body and stood up. "I am getting tired," she said. "I guess I will go to bed."

"No, wait a minute. What is it? Trouble with Warren?"

She stood there, looking down at her bare feet peeking out from under the long gown. She wiggled her toes. "No," she said. "Yes. I don't know. I don't understand him."

Her father said, "Oh."

"I mean, he doesn't . . . He didn't . . ."

"He didn't call you tonight?"

"Yes, but . . . It's not just that . . ." she looked away. "Everything was so nice. I just don't get it."

"Maybe he was busy," her father said casually.

"Yeah."

He stood up then and held her, resting his chin on the top of her head. He wanted to say look, Lee, Warren is only fifteen years old, you know, that's a time when "forever" can be three weeks . . . He wanted to say, please don't wear your heart on your sleeve that way, you'll only get hurt when you show you're that vulnerable . . . He wanted to say I swear to you, there will be many Warrens in your life, each one more wonderful than the last—for a while—

He didn't say any of it but he felt exhausted from the conversation he hadn't had. He wished Lee could enjoy the company of different people as he had begun to do, instead of fastening onto just one.

"Should I call him, Daddy?" Lee asked, her voice muffled against his shoulder.

"No. No, don't call him, Lee."

"Why not?"

"Honey, you know, there are lots of other boys besides Warren. It can be as much fun to see a lot of people instead of just one . . ."

She pulled away from him. "Oh," she said, "you just don't understand."

Lee was standing outside when Warren left Carroll's. She had been there since camp let out at 2:30. Her heart leaped a little as she saw the door open and Warren, in a blue workshirt and tan chinos, come out. She made herself smile.

"Hi, Warren!"

"Oh, hi, Lee."

"I was just going to the supermarket," she said, nodding toward the big store next door.

"Oh. I've got to pick up a prescription across the street . . ."

"Want me to come with you? My stuff can wait . . ."

"Um, well, sure, okay, if you want to . . ."

They walked across the street together. Lee's heart was pounding and she felt sick again. That wasn't Warren next to her. Warren would have said come to the store with me then we'll get a soda then I'll walk you home . . . Warren would have said boy is it great to see you after a long hot day . . . Warren would have his arm around her shoulder . . . Warren wouldn't be looking straight ahead and heading for the drug store as if it were a bomb shelter in an air attack . . . This Warren didn't speak at all. He went into the store and right over to the prescription counter, where the clerk nodded at him and indicated it would take a minute.

"How have you been?" Lee asked, as though it had been ages since she'd seen him. She succeeded in sounding casual but she was almost in tears.

"Good," he answered. "Real busy . . ."

"Me, too," she lied.

He took the prescription the clerk handed him and paid for it, turned and headed for the door. She had to take quick little steps to keep up with him. She wished he'd look at her.

"Eileen and Buff are going to the skating rink tonight," she said hurriedly. "Want to go?"

"Aw, no, I can't. My uncle and aunt are coming for dinner."

"Do you have to stay? After dinner, I mean?"

"Well, yeah, I really do . . . I don't get to see them that much."

"How about tomorrow?" she blurted and was instantly sorry. I'm making a fool of myself, she thought . . . But I know he'd feel the same way about me again if only he spent a little time with me, if only—

"Gee, I really can't, Lee, look, I'm in a rush, I'm sorry, I've really gotta hustle . . ."

And he was gone.

I hate him, she thought. I just hate him!

That night she called him. His mother answered the phone. She quickly covered the mouthpiece with her shirttail and asked for Warren in a voice his mother wouldn't recognize.

She listened to him say hello three times impatiently and hung up.

She made up a fantasy that he had received a telepathic message from her that would revive all the old feeling and he would call her right back.

She had counted all the way to 1000 when she gave up the fantasy.

A Friday morning.

"Hey, Alan! Long time no see! Gettin' much?"

"Stanley, has it ever struck you as appropriate that we always seem to meet in the men's room?" He continued to wash his hands without looking up.

"Ahhh-ha!" Stanley barked. "Love your sense of humor, listen, Alan, don't say no to me this time, I've been looking all over the damn office for you."

He wiped his hands and turned around. "Stan, come on," he said, smiling in spite of his exasperation. "I really don't need a matchmaker. Honestly. I appreciate all this consideration, but I'm handling my own social life just fine without—"

"Alan, wait. It's a favor I need. Please, you're the only guy who can help me out."

"Me?"

"Yeah. Look, Alan, it *does* have to do with a chick—no, don't walk away, hear me out, please?"

Alan Currie sighed and leaned back against the sink.

"Thanks." Stanley took a deep breath. "It's very complicated. See, I'm supposed to have my kids for three weeks every summer, right? Well, July was out because I was having my apartment painted and the air conditioner broke and I was staying with Harriet and this was the last—okay, okay, I'll get to the point. Anyway, now I have the kids, right? Only it turns out I've got to go out of town for four days while they're here and I just can't stick them with a babysitter, I can't take them with me, it's business,

Jeanette would have a fit, she's already on her own vacation in the Catskills, so what I figured would be the best solution—I'd call Jeanette's sister to come here and stay with them. You know, it's *family*, so it's not so bad that I'm not there—"

"Stan, this is really interesting, but I've got about a ton of work on my desk—"

"I'm almost *there*, Alan, just give me two more minutes. So I called Sally, she lives in Albany, works for the governor, and anyway, she said she'd come in, she'd take some time off, she loves the kids, you know . . ."

"Stanley, you're putting me to sleep."

". . . But I'd like to do something nice for her. I'd like her to have a nice date—look, it's all on me—it's just that she's doing this for me even though I'm not even in her family any more and I feel well, I feel guilty as hell for leaving this way, and Sally doesn't have that much fun and after all, this is the Big Apple, you can take her to—"

"Hold it. Hold it!" He pushed himself away from the sink, where he was beginning to feel cornered. "First of all, why *me*, Stan?"

Stanley inhaled again. "Look, Sally's a nice girl. You're the nicest guy I know."

"In other words, we're both dull, straight and boring."

"No." Stanley grew serious. "You're stable. You're grown up. You're kind. That's all, Alan. The people I run with, yeah, they're fun-loving, we close the bars seven nights a week. That's what I need, Alan, but you don't."

"So what's with your sister-in-law. She's not married?"

"My *ex*-sister-in-law. And no, she's not. She never has been."

"How old is she?"

"Thirty-five, thirty-six . . ."

"How come she's never been married?"

"She's not a dog, Alan, I swear. She's smart. Maybe that's it, she's too smart. She's too smart for *me*, Alan . . ."

He didn't speak the obvious. He just nodded, not sure what he was nodding at.

"It's just one night, Alan, and it's my treat. The whole evening, whatever you want to do, just make it nice. So she'll feel it was worth the trip. I want somebody nice for her, Alan. I like her. Even though I know she never cared much for me. Just like her sister!" He laughed. "So how about it, Alan? Huh?"

"Oh . . . sure, Stanley . . ."

"Fantastic, Alan, will you pick her up at the airport?"

Alan Currie threw his arms into the air and rolled his eyes in exasperation.

"My car," Stanley said. "You can take my car. It's in the garage in my building!"

When the phone rang at five o'clock, Lee raced for it. Warren. It had to be Warren! But it wasn't.

"Look, honey, something's come up . . . I've got to run out to LaGuardia for Mr. Ackerman and then I'll be going back into the city, so I'll be late tonight. Will you be all right?"

"Sure . . ."

"Why don't you call one of the girls?"

"No, Daddy, I'll be all right."

As soon as she hung up, the phone rang again. And again she was sure. Warren was missing her. Even if he called just to be polite, it would be something . . . She let it ring a few more times so he'd know she wasn't sitting there just waiting for him. Then she picked it up and tried her rehearsed "hello."

"Listen, Lee, I wanted you to hear it from me first," Connie began.

Lee closed her eyes.

"Warren was with Lynn Malesky at the skating rink last night. He's such a rat, really, you've got to watch those quiet ones—"

"Did Sam talk to him?" Lee asked. Her eyes were still closed and her stomach was hurting.

"Well, he just said hi and stuff. He wasn't going to get into anything . . ."

"Did he tell Sam why he stopped seeing me?" Each question hurt and embarrassed Lee to the point of tears but she had to ask.

"If he did, I don't know about it, Lee," Connie said.

"Would you tell me if he did, Connie?" she asked quietly.

"I swear I would, Lee," Connie said.

"This is lovely of you to pick me up, like this," Sally Post was saying as they drove away from the airport. ". . . A complete stranger . . ."

"Hey, listen, that's the best kind to pick up," he said and swung left onto the parkway.

Sally grinned. "I appreciate it."

"My pleasure. Stanley tells me you're with the governor."

"I'm rarely with the governor. That's part of the problem. My boss has the same complaint. I work for the comptroller."

"I see!" He looked over at her. So this was Stanley's sister-in-law. Ex. Without realizing it he began to shake his head slowly from side to side.

"What is it?" Sally asked.

"What's what?"

"Why are you shaking your head like that?"

He laughed. "I really didn't know I was doing that," he answered. "Actually, I was finding it hard to associate you with Stanley."

"Oh!" she cried. "Good."

He heard the sobbing from the bathroom as soon as he got through the apartment door. His buoyant mood vanished.

"Lee?" he called as he ran for the bathroom. "Lee? Open up now!" He pounded loudly.

"It's open," she gasped and he felt like a fool in a bad movie. He wiped his forehead and opened the door.

She was crouched on the floor next to the toilet. Her face was hidden by her arm but he could see her red cheeks and rumpled clothes. He sat down on the edge of the bathtub and stroked her damp hair.

He started to ask if Warren were responsible for this but it sounded so stuffy he choked back the words, deciding instead on "What happened?"

"He paid no attention to me for such a long time," Lee said, sobbing. ". . . But I kept thinking that if I could just talk to him and be with him for a little while he would see that he still liked me, that I could make him like me again . . . Or at least I could find out what I did to make him mad . . ." The tears began again.

Her father continued to stroke her hair. "You know," he said, leaning close to her, "this is your very first love. You won't believe me, but I promise there'll be more. Probably a lot more, honey. I _promise_ you this won't hurt so much after a little while . . ."

"Yes it will," she said firmly. "It'll always hurt. And I feel like I made such a big fool out of myself . . ."

"And you're the only one in the world who's ever

been hurt and felt like a fool. No one else ever did that or ever will!"

"Oh, Daddy," she said, resting her head against his shoulder, "what'll I do when I'm in New York and away from you? You can make things seem all right even when they're not and you never say 'I told you so . . .'"

She couldn't see his frown. For the first time he concentrated on how he would feel when she moved out. He needed her as much as she needed him. He shook his head, as if to clear it. He wanted her! He did! But again the thought: the waves it would make! And how could he put the burden on her—a child having to choose. Wouldn't it seem as though he were turning her against her mother?

A few minutes later he asked at Lee's bedroom door if he might tuck her in. The question made her smile for the first time that day.

"Daddy," she whispered, as she hugged his neck, "I want to stay with you. I don't want to go to New York. Don't make me go. Please."

He pulled back and looked at her. "How about your mother?" he asked softly.

She didn't even pause. "I don't get along well with Mom," she said. "But it isn't that. It isn't that I want to hurt her. It's that I'd rather be with you. Can I?"

He couldn't give her an answer. She must know that the two of them couldn't make the decision by themselves. And he couldn't raise her hopes. Or his.

"You sure?" he asked and when she nodded solemnly, he said, "Let me think it all out."

"And then—?"

"No promises. I can't make them, Lee . . ." He leaned over and kissed her forehead. "I love you," he said, and stood up.

"I love you, too, Daddy," she whispered.

Nine

"Joel's just going to sleep most of the day, Allison," her mother said, touching her hand.

"He's really fine, Allie," her father added. "You didn't need to skip both your classes today. Your mother and I are here . . ." The three sat together in the waiting room on Joel's hospital floor.

Allison didn't look at either of her parents. She sat on the brown naugahyde couch with her knees pressed together. Occasionally, she played with her fingers. Her parents, sitting on either side of her, began to talk over her head.

"Where's Lee?" her mother wanted to know.

"At camp."

"Did she say she'd call or anything?"

"She's not in a great mood these days, Elaine, she's having some problems with her boyfriend."

"Oh, is she? What kind of problems?"

He coughed and uncrossed his legs. He didn't want to discuss Lee and Warren. He had a vague feeling that would be betraying Lee's confidence, even though this was Lee's mother; but he didn't want to talk about that. He wanted to talk about something else.

"Elaine, let's just take a walk down the hall for a moment, okay? Will you excuse us, Allie?" He looked at her as he stood up, but she was staring straight ahead.

"Allison?" he said.

"Huh?"

"I want to talk to your mother, okay? We'll be right back."

"Okay . . ."

Her mother stood up and followed him. "What is it?" she asked. "What's the matter?"

He took her arm and quickened his step as he spoke.

"Lee has asked if she can continue to stay with me after the summer's over."

Elaine Currie stopped walking. "What?"

"You heard me, Elaine. You must have considered the possibility at some time or another . . ."

"I never considered it," she said flatly. "I never thought about it. We agreed it would be for the summer. I stand by my agreements."

He almost smiled. "I'm going to let that pass, Elaine," he said.

"Oh, Alan, you know what I mean . . ."

"I want you to think about it. I'm thinking of Lee's best interests. You know how it's been with you two, Elaine, just bad chemistry. Maybe in time . . ."

"I never should have consented to her staying the summer."

"Consented! That's ridiculous, Elaine. I'm her father. I have rights, too. It's not entirely up to you, you know. Now, all I wanted to do was put the idea in your mind." He cocked his head. "Let's get back to Allison, she's all alone over there." He walked ahead of his ex-wife and sat down heavily next to Allison, who didn't seem to notice either of them approaching.

"I'm thinking of what's best for Lee, you know," her mother said after some minutes. "For *all* the kids."

He whirled in his seat. "What the hell do you think *I'm* thinking of, waterskiing on Lake Michigan?"

"Don't be sarcastic, Alan—"

"Well, don't you imply—"

"*Stop it!*" Allison doubled over between them, her hands covering her ears.

Brought up short, they reached for her.

"Allie, Allie, we're sorry, baby," her father murmured.

"It's all right, honey," her mother said.

Allison sat up abruptly. "Don't you care anything about Joel?" she demanded. "He's the one who matters now, he's lying there with doctors cutting him—what if they make a mistake, huh? What if he got hurt?"

"Hey—Allie—they're not going to—Allison, that's worrying needlessly, honey. A tonsillectomy is just routine for the doctors. Honestly."

"Well, not for Joel, and you two are arguing and yelling again just as if we weren't even in a hospital, waiting for—"

"All right." Her father stopped her by taking her face in his hands. "Okay. No more arguing." He looked over at her mother. "No more fighting."

The little girl reached up and hugged Lee's neck.

Lee smiled. "'Bye, Lily. See you tomorrow . . ." Her smile faded as the little girl disappeared into the camp bus.

"Come on, Lee," Connie said, tugging Lee's arm. "Let's go to the beach and relax."

"Let's get something to eat first," Virginia suggested.

"No . . . No, not me," Lee said. "You go ahead . . ."

Virginia stopped walking and put her hands on her hips. "Oh, Lee," she said. "That's what you said yesterday and the day before. Sorry, but you're coming with us."

Lee stopped walking, too. "I don't feel like it," she said and shook her head.

"Listen," Virginia said, "what happened with Warren was a bummer and he's Scuzzy Rat Number One, but you can't go into retirement, Lee. You're acting just like Eileen's mother."

That made Lee smile and she hid her face. "I feel so dumb," she said into her hands. "I was such an idiot, I don't know how you can even talk to me."

Connie said, *"That's* being an idiot, you idiot."

Both girls took Lee's hands and began to pull her toward their bicycles. "Okay," Connie said. "First food, then beach."

"No . . ." Lee said, stopping them. "I really don't feel like it. I just want to go home."

"Don't let her, Connie," Virginia said. "We're not letting you, that's all. We're going to the beach and you'll meet some great new guy and forget all about Warren!"

"Oh, no," Lee said angrily. "Not any more. It's not worth it, getting involved with a boy. I'm finished with the whole thing."

"My heart!" Virginia clutched her chest and pretended to fall backward. "You're only fifteen. Think what you'll be missing later when you find out about sex!"

Connie laughed. "Cut it out, Gin, she's serious," she said.

"I am," Lee said. "I am serious. Nothing lasts. Look at all of us and our parents. All you do is get hurt and I just don't want to go through this again for anything!" She got on her bike and rode off before the girls could say any more.

She went straight home.

Instead of cheering her, the sunlight streaming into the empty apartment deepened her loneliness. Part of her wished she had gone with the girls but the other part knew why she hadn't. She was still hoping that the phone would ring and it would be Warren. Warren saying he missed her, that the other girl only made him realize how much he wanted to be with Lee.

She knew now that it wouldn't happen. She knew it was only a fantasy. But fantasies are so hard to shake; and if she didn't stay home, she'd never know if it might come true.

With a sigh, Elaine Currie picked up the phone on her desk, began to dial, and then hung up. She had wanted to handle this alone; she'd put off calling him for days, thinking it was her imagination, hoping it would dissipate.

Allison was becoming a problem. Of all the family—Allison! The stable one, the sweet one, the most reliable, the least argumentative.

Elaine Currie bit down on her lower lip. It wasn't her imagination. She dialed again and this time, stayed on.

"Mr. Currie, please," she said to the secretary, and took a deep breath while she waited for him to answer.

"Hello, Alan," she said and went on in a rush. "I'm sorry to bother you at the office, but I can't call from home where Allison can hear me. I'm at my office."

"What office?"

"My office. At Je Suis Cosmetics. I told you."

He cut her off. "What's this about Allison not hearing you?"

She bit her lip again. "Allison's changed since Joel's come home. Well, it was happening before, I guess, but it's worse now. A lot worse. I mean . . . I just took for granted all the little ways she had of taking over the house, you know the way Allison is, it made it easy on me and she liked it and I just didn't give it as much thought as I should . . ."

"Give what as much thought?"

"She's stopped taking her classes. Just refuses to go. At first it was because she had to take care of Joel while he was recuperating, but he's fine now, so she takes him to the bus for camp and then she comes home."

"What does she do at home?" he asked.

"Cleaning," she answered. "She cleans. She vacuums. Dusts. Mops. She shops, she does laundry. She cooks . . ."

"She's taken over your job?"

"Now, Alan, don't do that. There are plenty of working women whose children don't turn into domestic servants. I've made it clear to her that I want her to go back to school . . . I can handle the housework, Alan—"

"All right, I'm sorry," he said.

"I'm really worried about her," she went on. "She seems so withdrawn. And it's almost as if she resents me when I do get home."

"Maybe she should see somebody," he said. "A doctor."

"That's what I was thinking . . ."

"Maybe Joel's operation threw her. Allie has a sensitive nature. Maybe her way of getting her feelings out is to be helpful around the house."

"Maybe. I'll look into therapy for her and get back to you. I'm glad you suggested it . . . that we're in agreement."

"Fine, Elaine." He paused and then changed the subject. "Have you thought about what we discussed at the hospital?"

"About Lee staying with you."

"You know how much better she is with me, you know that."

She knew. But she didn't want to argue now. "How is she?" she asked.

"You mean right now? Kind of mopey."

"Still the boyfriend?" She took a breath. This was something she could discuss with Lee, wanted to discuss with Lee. They were both women, she could handle that better than Alan—

A thought struck her.

"Alan? Suppose Allison spends the weekend with you. Alone. And you have Lee come here. I'll invite her. It'll get Allison out of the house and away from Joel and all the responsibilities she's taken on and it'll give me a chance to talk to Lee."

"And give Lee a chance to talk to *you*."

"Yes . . . What do you think?"

"All right . . . I'd love to have Allie."

"And I'd have Joel here, he'd get to be taken care of by his real mother," she said, "and . . . I'd really like to try . . . with Lee."

"Fair enough."

"Why don't you pick Allison up here Friday after work?"

"Yes," he said, "I could do that. I could bring Lee in with me Friday morning. I'll have her take a day off from camp and she could spend some time with Allison before Joel comes home. How about that? That might be good for both of them."

When her mother called that night inviting her for the weekend, Lee was immediately suspicious and said so.

"Why do you want to see me?" she asked. She wasn't sure what her mother knew, either about her wish to stay with her father or about her experience with Warren. "Is it about anything . . . special?"

"No!" her mother answered quickly. "I want to see my daughter. I want to be with my daughter, is that unusual?"

"No . . ."

"I do, Lee. But in a way, this visit has more to do with your sister than with you."

"What?"

"Your sister is having some problems, and both of us could use some maturity and compassion from you. I know you haven't spent much time with her this summer so you don't know all that's been happening . . ."

Lee felt a pang. She hadn't spent all her time thinking about the fact that her family was scattered and fragmented; occasionally something hit her and it was usually hard and it hurt. But she'd been so involved with her own problems she hadn't thought about Allison at all.

"What's wrong with Allison?" she asked.

Her mother told her briefly. "So besides giving us time together," she finished, "it will give Allison some much-needed time with her father and above all, get her out of the house and away from Joel. I'm asking for your cooperation, Lee . . ."

Of course, she couldn't say no.

Ten

Lee and her father reached the offices of WNVL a little before nine on Friday. His secretary was waiting for him.

"Hi, Betty, you remember my daughter, Lee?" he said.

Betty smiled. "Welcome to the madhouse, Lee. Listen, Alan, Joan just called. The White House has asked for air time tonight."

He groaned. "What time?"

"Not sure. They're guessing nine. That's what he always gets."

Lee left them and wandered down the hall. She came to a series of small cubicles with a sign at the entrance reading "Writers' Den." She poked her head around a partition and recognized Grace Raphael's back.

Lee hadn't thought of Grace Raphael for weeks.

She wasn't sure her father had, either; he had been talking about someone named Sally whom he'd met at the airport.

Grace was busy at her desk and didn't notice Lee, so Lee stood there for a moment watching her. "A dog" was what Lee had called her the night of the party, that wonderful-awful party where she'd first met Warren. Grace certainly wasn't a dog. She was pretty, and she'd tried to be nice to Lee that night.

Grace wasn't a threat any more. Lee called her name softly.

Grace whirled around in her little swivel chair. "Lee! Hi! How are you?" she asked.

Encouraged by the greeting, Lee smiled and stepped into the cubicle.

"Awful," she answered. "You?"

"Oh . . . muddling through. Have a seat." Grace reached over and pulled a pile of papers off the one remaining chair in her little space. She dumped the papers on the floor and Lee laughed.

"Are you busy?" Lee asked.

"Sure. But I'd rather talk to you. What's new?"

Lee looked down at her lap. She wanted Grace to ask her the right questions; she didn't want to volunteer. Not yet.

"Boyfriend?" Grace asked. It was the right question.

"No more," she said, still looking down.

"Me, too," Grace said and smiled.

Lee felt warmed. She'd have been embarrassed to

have this conversation with anyone else; but Grace was a stranger. They'd probably never meet again. And somehow she knew Grace understood what she was feeling.

"Were you in love with my father?" Lee asked boldly.

Grace smiled again and shrugged. "I really didn't know him long enough to love him, Lee," she said sincerely. "He hasn't been separated that long and he needs time to get back on his feet. I think I was his first date, as a matter of fact."

Lee nodded. "Yes, you were," she said.

"Well, you see?"

"No," Lee said frankly. "I don't. All I see is things don't last between people . . . Feelings don't last."

Grace leaned back in her chair and regarded Lee.

"Lots of times feelings don't last, Lee," she said. "Especially when you're fourteen—"

"Fifteen," Lee said stiffly.

"Fifteen, too," Grace said. "I know I probably sound patronizing, but it's true. A real love, mature love, has to come when you're older, it's just the way things work. You're supposed to have a lot of loves when you're young to prepare you for the real thing."

"Well, my parents were older," Lee countered. "And that didn't last, either. And neither did my best friends' parents . . ."

Grace nodded slowly. "I don't know what to tell you, Lee," she said. "Except that just because some marriages break up doesn't mean they all do. And sometimes a second marriage works out great because the people involved really know what they want by that time."

Lee sighed.

"Listen, honey, I'm no expert, I've never been married. But I've—"

"Here you are!"

Both Grace and Lee looked up to see Lee's father in the doorway of the cubicle.

"I've been looking all over the office for you," he said.

"Sorry, Daddy." Lee stood up. "I was just saying hello to Grace."

"Grace, did you get the word about the President's speech?" he asked.

She nodded. "I was just seeing what we could pull if it's nine o'clock."

"Good. Come on, honey, let Grace get back to work now." He looked at Grace. "I'll be back when we get official word." He put his hand on Lee's shoulder and walked her back down the hall toward his own office. "What were you and Grace talking about?" he asked casually.

"You," Lee answered just as casually.

He stopped walking. "Really?" He was frowning.

"Not really," she said, making a face at him. "Just girl talk." She began to walk again.

"Now you're talking 'girl talk,'" he muttered. "Used to be when I brought you to my office you'd be content with the colored pens and 'Happy the Clown.' "

Lee arrived at her mother's apartment at ten-thirty and rang the bell.

"Hi," Allison said quietly as she opened the door.

"Don't sound so glad to see me. Can I come in?"

"Sure. I'm sorry." Allison stepped back, letting her sister enter.

Lee deposited her bag on the floor. "Joel in camp?" She knew he was.

"Uh-huh. I'm in the middle of some—" she glanced around the living room, "—some cleaning up. Want something to eat?"

"No, you don't have to play hostess with me."

"I wasn't."

"Okay . . ."

Allison turned and returned to her chore of putting books back on shelves.

Lee went over to the couch and sat down. "Hey," she said. "We've got all day together. Want to do something?"

Allison shrugged. "I've got stuff to do . . ."

"That's Mother's stuff. Let's go out."

"Well, we have to go out later anyway . . . Mom thought it might be nice for me to show you the high school. It's not far from here . . ." She bent down and picked up more books.

Lee tilted her head. "What do you mean, show me the school?" she asked.

"It's starting soon. Labor Day's next week and then it starts right after that."

"Well, so what?"

"So Mom thought that maybe if you saw what the school looked like then it wouldn't be this scary unknown thing. You know . . ." Allison put the last of the books away and walked into the kitchen. Lee followed her.

"Listen, she never mentioned anything about visiting any school when she invited me here," Lee said angrily.

"Don't get mad, Lenore. It was only to make you feel better about it, that's all. Mom thought maybe you were worried about starting a new school. I mean, anybody would be. I am. Joel is. And as long as you're here you could have a chance to look at it."

"Great!" Lee threw her hands in the air. "Just great. Some trick!"

Allison began to take bowls and pans out of the cabinets.

Lee whirled around. "Allie, what—are—you—doing?"

"Getting dinner ready."

"At ten-thirty in the morning?"

Allison was calm. "I'm just getting everything ready, that's all."

"You don't have to do that. You won't even be here. Mom and I'll do it. Put it away, Allison."

Allison didn't answer, but Lee could see her lips tighten. She continued to put things on the counter.

Lee felt contrite. Allison really wasn't the same girl she'd known at home. "Allie . . . let me help you. Okay?"

Her sister stopped and looked at her. "It's meat loaf," she said. "I'm putting it in the pan now, so all we have to do is bake it later."

"Well . . . Show me what to do."

Allison was still staring at her and Lee felt uncomfortable.

"Want to cut up an onion?" she asked.

Lee inhaled. "I hate knives, you know that . . ."

Allison turned and went back to work.

"All right, I'll try it," Lee said. She took the cutting board off the wall and shivered as she slid a knife out of its wooden holder. She held it gingerly and picked up the onion. It took her nearly five minutes to peel the onion and cut one slice, and her eyes were tearing badly.

Allison smiled slightly and Lee realized how long it had been since she'd seen her sister smile. Allison used to smile all the time, she thought.

"I'll do it," Allison said, taking the knife from Lee.

Allison did the entire meat loaf and then proceeded to clean the kitchen. Lee watched her pull out rags, cleaning solutions, waxes. She felt useless, bored.

"Gee," she said casually, "you could get a good job

in somebody's house as a domestic, Allison. Daddy and I should hire you!"

"This is my own house," Allison said. "And somebody has to keep it nice."

"What about friends?" Lee asked.

Allison put down her rag. "We should go over to the school, Lenore," she said.

Lee brushed the idea aside. "I'm serious, Allison. Joel's in camp all day, Mother's at work. Why aren't you out with some kids or something?"

"I don't know any kids."

"You do so. Daddy says you met some nice kids in your summer class. And why'd you stop going to that, anyway? Don't you know now you'll just have to take seventh-grade math over again?"

"This is J-Joel's last day at camp," Allison stammered, close to tears. "And then I'll have to be here full time anyway. Besides, it's none of your business, leave me alone."

"Well, my school is none of your business, either," Lee said, feeling mean.

"You're right, and I don't care if you go or not!" Allison said loudly, beginning to cry.

Lee quickly went to her sister and put her arms around her. "Allie, Allie, I'm sorry. I really am."

Allison fought to stop crying, wiping her eyes with the tail of her shirt and with her fists.

"I just wish everyone would leave me alone. I'm not hurting anyone. I'm just taking care of everything, that's all."

"I'll leave you alone, Allie. But I'm going on record saying I'm worried about you. Look: we're all alone here in the city. Two sisters. How often does this ever happen? Let's *do* something! Let's go out. Please? Let's walk around. I don't know how you stand staying cooped up—all right, all right—" She held up her palms as she saw Allison's expression. "I won't talk about that but I want to get out of here and I want you to come with me. Please?"

Allison looked around the apartment.

"It's clean!" Lee yelled. "It's so spotless you could lick it! Now, come on!"

They went to the Central Park Zoo. They watched the seals being fed. They laughed at the seals' diving tricks as they went for each fish and the way they applauded themselves when they caught them. They bought each other balloons. They saw the elephants, apes and birds. They watched the antics of a mother polar bear and her cub.

They walked to Broadway and looked in the shops at the strange and funny souvenirs. They tried on rubber masks and electric buzzers that you hide in your palm until you shake hands with someone.

They looked at all the people on line for cheaper theatre tickets and tried to guess which show each person wanted to see. Then they'd run up to the ticket window and listen to see if their guesses were right.

When they got hungry they bought hot dogs and

orange drinks from a street vendor and ate them under the statue of George M. Cohan.

"Allison," Lee said, her mouth full of hot dog. "Remember how when Daddy moved out of the house you never said anything?"

"What do you mean, I never said anything? I asked them a lot of things . . ."

"I don't mean that. I mean, I was yelling a lot, right?"

Allison nodded. "Yes, you blamed Mom. You screamed at her all the time."

"I was scared, too. And so was Joel, remember?"

"I think I've gotten him over that," Allison said defensively.

"But I mean, you never said anything. You were calm all the time. You listened to Mother, you patted her on the back, you were always hugging Daddy . . . and Joel . . . and me, too. Remember?"

"So?"

"Didn't you want Daddy and Mother to stay together? I could never figure out how you felt."

"I guess I did," Allison said. "But I knew they wouldn't and now I'm used to it."

"What's it like living with Mother by herself?"

Allison shrugged and sipped her soda. "We don't see her that much. Just at night and then she's tired and I have things to do, give Joel his bath and get dinner and do dishes and put Joel to bed . . ."

"Doesn't Mother do any of that?"

"She doesn't have to. I like to do it."

"It's like . . . your house. And you're the mommy and the daddy, right?"

"Well, in a way," Allison said lightly.

"What about me?" Lee asked.

"What *about* you?"

"Well, I suppose you've got it all figured out where *I* fit in . . ."

"I don't know, Lenore," Allison said. "You fit into your own life. We're all different now." She looked at her watch. "We have to pick up Joel at four."

"That's over an hour from now!"

"I know . . ."

"Well, look, just so we don't get into too much of a hassle about that, why don't we walk over to the school you were going to show me. Okay?"

"Okay."

Looking at the school would be all right, Lee decided. She didn't have to go in. *Anything* to keep Allison from going back to that apartment!

"Joelly!" Allison cried and ran to him. She had been craning her neck to find him among all the little blue shorts and white tee shirts that got off the camp bus. "Hi, sweetie." Then: "What happened to your eye?"

"Wendy hit me with the softball."

Allison frowned. "It's all purple . . ."

Joel brightened. "Frank, my counselor? He said it'd turn purple *and* yellow!"

Allison hugged him. "I'll put some ice on it when we get home . . ."

"Noo-oo—"

"Look, Joelly, Lenore's here!" Allison said, distracting him.

Joel turned and looked at where Allison was pointing. He didn't say anything.

"Hi, Joel!" Lee called and came over to them. "Hey, that's a super-looking shiner!"

Joel broke into a grin.

Their mother got back to the apartment only ten minutes before their father arrived. She was breathless and apologetic. She hugged Lee, fussed over Joel's black eye, and complimented Allison, although with slightly less enthusiasm, on the aromatic odor of meat loaf.

When the buzzer rang, she called, "Allison, it's Daddy! Get your suitcase!" and hurried over to let him in.

He stood in the doorway and looked around. "Nice," he said. "First time I've gotten a good look at the inside. Not bad for the price."

"Come in." She closed the door behind him.

"Daddy, Daddy!" Joel bounded into his arms. "Look at my black eye! Don't I look like a boxer? You know what Alexander did? He took charcoal out of Arts and Crafts and drew it all around his eye to make it look like mine! And then Henry wanted it and Billy, and Wendy wanted me to hit her with a softball back, so she could have—"

His father was laughing and hugging him. "Let me see, let me see," he said. "Oh, boy, that's some mouse, kiddo! What happened?"

"I *told* you, Wendy hit me, are you gonna stay, Daddy?"

"No, sport, no, I'm here to pick up your sister. Each of you guys is going to have your own special weekend with Daddy, all by yourselves, and this one'll be Allison's, okay? Next weekend—yours."

Joel stayed in his father's arms, but pulled away. "*I* want to go this weekend. Let *Allison* go next time."

"Naw, we kind of think it's best for Allison to come this time. You know, she's been working very hard, taking care of you and Mom and the house . . . You—" he poked Joel lightly in the stomach, "—you had camp and you got to have fun all day, right?"

He put Joel down.

"Hi, Dad." Lee came over and kissed him.

"Have a nice day with Allie?" he asked, returning the kiss.

"Uh-huh."

"Where is she? Allison?"

"Allison!" her mother called. "Your father's here!"

Allison appeared in the doorway of her room. "Hi," she murmured.

"Hi, there, big girl! All set?"

"I'm not going, Daddy."

Her mother spun around. "Allison!" she cried.

"I'm not. I'm sorry, Daddy, I just . . . can't."

Mother and father exchanged looks.

"Come on, Allie," her father said, going toward her. "Let's talk in your room."

They went in and closed the door.

Her mother turned to Lee. "Did she say anything to you about this?" she demanded.

Lee widened her eyes and shrugged. "No," she answered, but when her mother continued to glare at her, she snapped, "She didn't. I swear."

"What's wrong, baby?" her father asked, sitting down next to her on the bed. "Tell me. Is it me? Are you sore at me?"

"No! No, Daddy, no!"

"Well, then?"

She didn't answer.

"Look, Allie—I planned a nice time for us. Just us two. Dinner here in the city, then home, then tomorrow shopping together—whatever you'd like to do. Swimming, boating, movies—anything, Allie. Just you and me."

"But, Daddy—"

"What?"

She nearly whispered. "I just don't want to leave Joel here," she managed.

He didn't blow up as she'd feared. "Allison, he's

got his mother here. And Lee. You need some time away."

"No, I don't, I don't!" Then she was crying. "I feel better when I can take care—I mean, when I'm with Joel. There's so much he doesn't—I mean, only I can—"

He touched her shoulder. "You think you're the only one who understands him, right?"

"Well, I am," she said evenly. "He tells me things he doesn't tell anyone else. And Mom never has time to fix his things, you know, his models, and listen to everything he says . . ."

Her father sat back and folded his hands. He looked over at Allison and back down at his hands. It was a while before he spoke.

"Okay," he said finally. "What if Joel comes, too?"

She smiled. "Would you really take him, too? Not me alone?" she asked almost shyly.

"Yes," he said, nodding. "Sure." He stood up. "You packed?"

"No . . ."

"Get packed. I'll pack Joel."

"*I'll*—"

"No, *I* will. You take care of yourself."

Lee didn't realize how tightly her teeth were clenched as she watched her mother kiss Joel and Allison goodbye and close the door behind them and her father. She turned her back and stared straight ahead at a wall, trying to control the tension that had been building inside her.

"Well," she heard her mother say, "what did you think? Did you see what I meant on the phone?"

Lee blinked. She'd forgotten for a moment what her mother was talking about. Oh, yes: Allison. Allison's strange behavior. She swallowed, but didn't speak.

"Lee? Didn't you see her? The dinner? The way she refused to go with her father?"

Lee turned around stiffly. She knew her face was red, it felt so hot . . .

"What I saw was another trick on your part, Mother. What was that business about seeing the high school? You never mentioned *that* in your phone call about my compassion and maturity!"

"Oh!" Her mother looked confused. "Lee, that was just an afterthought! Really! To give you something to do with your sister while you were here. Something to get her out of the house. And of course, just so you might feel more . . . at home with the idea—"

As she broke off, it was Lee's turn to feel confused. She'd been feeling angry and betrayed since that morning when Allison had told her about visiting the school. She'd been ready to believe her mother had tricked her. Now she wasn't so sure, but she wasn't ready to give up her anger. She snorted.

Her mother crossed the room and held Lee's shoulders. "It's the truth! I never even had it in mind when I spoke to you. It occurred to me you might like to see it before you went there!"

"I don't want to go there!" Lee cried shrilly.

Her mother let go of her then, and Lee felt sick. She knew how she sounded—how she always sounded whenever she faced her mother, but she didn't know why. And she couldn't stop herself.

"Lee?" her mother said. Her tone was different. "Come on over and sit here with me on the couch."

Reluctantly, Lee sat. But she sat right on the edge and her back was very straight. "I don't want to go to that school," she repeated. "I want to stay with—I want to stay in Long Beach."

"Your father did tell me you'd . . . mentioned that. But you know, we did agree—"

"I don't care what we agreed then. Maybe I thought if I could just get the summer then everything else would take care of itself. I don't know, I don't know what I thought. I just want to stay with Daddy!" Lee listened to herself speaking the words as if she were standing outside her own body, watching as an impartial spectator. She hadn't wanted to hurt her mother; she hadn't wanted to bring up the subject of staying in Long Beach—she was too afraid of it; she hadn't even asked her father if he'd said anything about it. And here she was, doing the opposite of everything she'd planned.

She didn't think that her mother might be just as afraid of this discussion.

"Lee . . . Honey . . ." Her mother leaned forward, toward her. "Let's not talk about this right now. Please . . . It's so disturbing . . . especially when it was all talked out last spring . . . Look: there's something else I want to talk to you about. Okay? I'd really like you to tell me—that is, if you feel like talking about it—tell me about your boyfriend? I mean, don't you think it would help a little? You know, to talk to another woman?"

Lee knew that her mother was deliberately changing the subject, which was all right with her, but the subject she'd picked wasn't. She'd already talked to "another woman," a better authority, Lee knew, and a younger one, besides; someone who was more in tune with today.

"It'll help to talk about it, I think," her mother repeated.

Suddenly Lee was afraid and suspicious again. What had her father said about Warren?

"What do you know about it?" she snapped at her mother.

"Nothing!" Her mother drew back. "I don't know anything. Your father mentioned you were seeing someone and that you were mopey lately because things weren't going well."

Lee licked her upper lip with the tip of her tongue and turned away.

"Lee, I'm your mother! Look at me! I want to know what's happening in your life! Do you really think I wouldn't understand?"

That was exactly what Lee thought. She sniffed the air. "What's that?" she asked.

"Oh, Lord, it's Allison's meat loaf—" Her mother jumped up and ran for the kitchen. Lee followed slowly and got to the door in time to see her mother pulling a blackened, smoking pan from the oven. With a huge sigh, she put it down in the sink and gave a short laugh. "I felt guilty just now," she said with a smile to Lee. "I thought: Allison will kill me."

"Let's just make eggs," Lee said unenthusiastically.

"All right." Her mother opened the refrigerator door. "Won't you tell me anything, Lee?" she asked as she fumbled for the eggs and butter. "I do care about . . ."

Lee waved a hand as if to brush away the question. "It wasn't anything. I was just pretty stupid and I won't be that way again. That's all."

"What do you mean, stupid?"

"Just *stupid*, that's all!"

Her mother began to beat the eggs. She poured them into the frying pan, and in a few minutes, mother and daughter sat silently opposite each other at the kitchen table over steaming plates of scrambled eggs and rye toast. Lee knew her mother was trying to catch her eye but she wouldn't look up. She kept shoveling forkfuls of eggs into her mouth. They tasted awful.

"Lee?"

"What?"

"I'd like to know what you meant before. About being 'stupid.' "

"It doesn't matter. Forget it."

"I—I think—" Her mother was stammering. Lee wished she'd drop it. "There's so much I want to talk with you about . . ." she said hesitatingly. "It just seems that every time we're together there's so much to cover in so little time . . ."

"What do you mean?" Lee asked, but she didn't want to know. She didn't want to talk any more.

"Tell me something," her mother said. She put her elbows on the table and looked directly at Lee. She sounded to Lee as if she were on firmer ground now.

"Tell you what?"

"Do you know about—you know—things to use?"

Now Lee looked at her, frowning. "I don't know what you mean," she said.

"Things to *use. You* know . . . For birth control."

"What?" Lee's frown deepened; her mouth was open.

"Do you know about it," her mother said levelly. "I mean, we've never talked about it, you and I. It *is* important for every girl to—"

Lee stood up and slammed her fork down on the table. It clattered to the floor.

"You just don't know anything—" she shrieked, "about *anything!* There's this person you made up whose name is Lenore Currie but just doesn't happen to have anything to do with me at all!"

"Lee—" her mother called after her, but Lee didn't turn around. She ran into Allison's room and slammed the door. She felt embarrassed, misread, misunderstood and above all, angry. Again. Still. She lay down on the extra bed and cried very quietly so her mother wouldn't hear.

Her mother went into her own sleeping area when she realized that Lee would not be coming out again. She sat down at the little desk where she did her school work, buried her face in her hands and cried, very quietly so her daughter wouldn't hear.

Eleven

Slowly, quietly Lee turned the door handle and tiptoed out of Allison's room. It was only nine-thirty by the bedside clock, but the apartment was dark. Relieved, Lee slipped back into her sister's room, picked up the bag she had never unpacked, and crept to the front door.

I'm always sneaking out of here! The thought popped into her mind as she stood in the hall. It made her guilty, anxious and terribly lonely.

This time she took a taxi. There was a train to Long Beach twenty minutes after she got to Penn Station. She bought a *People* magazine and read it while she waited. She stayed near the information booth where the crowd congregated and when it was time to walk to her train she stayed close to a group going in the same direction. Her father had told her to try not to look as if she were alone in New York, especially at night.

The train ride was less than forty-five minutes.

She and a middle-aged man were the only ones to get off at Long Beach. The man walked from the train directly to a car where a woman was sitting in the driver's seat waiting for him. Lee could see her clearly when the front door opened and the light went on. The woman smiled and leaned over to kiss the man. His wife? Lee thought at first, of course it's his wife, and then, no . . . maybe it's not, it doesn't have to be, does it? It could be a girlfriend, it could be his sister, it could be anybody.

She began to shiver a little, though the night air was warm. She didn't know what to do next.

She looked around the empty platform and thought of her father spending the night here—waiting for her to get off the train. Tonight he was with Allison. And Joel. And Lee knew she would not and could not interfere with their time together, no matter how badly she wanted her room and her bed and her panda.

Or is that just an excuse, she thought. Am I too afraid to go home and face Daddy?

She smiled slightly. If it is an excuse, it's a good one, anyway.

There was a phone booth on the platform and Lee slipped into it and dialed Eileen's number. She hung up on the tenth ring. Friday night, she realized. Eileen was with her dad. Or her mom . . .

Ginny. I'll call Virginia. If she's not there, maybe Connie will be. *One* of us has to be home this weekend, just because of the odds!

Virginia herself picked up the phone when it had barely rung, though at first, Lee didn't recognize her voice.

"Gin?" she asked tentatively.

"Lee? Oh, Lee, is that you? Are you in the city?"

"No, I'm at the station. I took a train. What's wrong, how'd you know I was—"

"I called you. I was calling all afternoon and night. I finally got your father, he said he brought the other kids home and you were—oh, Lee—"

"Is your mother there?" she asked because Virginia sounded hysterical and Lee wondered if her friend were alone.

"No." Virginia sniffled loudly. "Why?"

"Do you want me to come over there?"

"Yes! Oh, yes, please, Lee, that's why I was calling. I just need—Eileen's away, you were away, Connie's out with Sam, I just feel so—"

"I'll be there as soon as I can, but I have to take a bus, Gin, my father doesn't even know I'm here and my mother doesn't know I left."

"Oh, Lee, life's such a mess . . ."

"I'll get a bus . . ."

"No, take a cab. I can pay him when you get here if you don't have the money."

"I don't. Okay, I'll cab it."

Virginia was waiting outside when Lee's taxi pulled up and she paid the driver. She pulled Lee and her suitcase up the walk and into the house. Lee stared at her friend's matted hair and tear-streaked face.

"Where's your mother?"

"She's out."

"What happened to you?"

Virginia slammed the door behind them both and turned to face Lee. "You know who she's out with?"

"How would I know?" Lee asked.

"She's out with her fiancé, that's who. She's getting married. She made the big announcement this afternoon."

"*What?*" Lee's jaw dropped. Virginia began to cry. "*Who?* Who's she marrying? You never even said she was *seeing* anyone, you always said she never even stuck to one man longer than—"

"I know what I said. That's what I thought, that's what she *told* me. How was I supposed to know she's a big liar, I believed her!" She was sobbing.

"Now, wait a second, wait a second," Lee said, going to her. "Are you telling me that your mother has been seeing someone all this time, someone that she now plans to marry, and you never even had an idea of it, Ginny? Do you have a tissue around here?"

"Over there." Virginia pointed. "Anyway, it's not exactly like that."

"What do you mean, not exactly like that? Here." Lee handed Virginia a pink Kleenex.

"She hasn't been seeing someone all this time."

"I don't get it," Lee said.

"She's only known him three weeks." Virginia blew her nose.

"I don't *believe* it! Three weeks!"

Virginia nodded. "She says he's the best thing that ever happened to her."

Lee sat down on the arm of Virginia's chair. "Did she introduce you?" she asked, "or will she wait until he moves in here and you bump into him in the bathroom. 'Oh, pardon me, I just noticed there's an extra toothbrush in here and it's marked *permanent,* could that be yours by any chance?' "

"Yeah, she introduced me to him. This afternoon. And he's not moving in with us. We're moving in with him. She says I'll just love farm life."

"Farm life?"

"Not exactly farm. Just a few hundred acres up in Connecticut. Oh, Lee—"

Lee swallowed. "Connecticut—" she whispered. She looked down at Virginia, wiping her eyes with a sopping-wet tissue. "Did she go out and leave you like this tonight?"

"Uh-uh." Virginia shook her head. "I wouldn't give her the satisfaction of watching me cry. That's reserved for my friends."

"What did you say to her, then?"

"Nothing."

"Nothing?"

"Yes, nothing. She wanted me to go out with them tonight to celebrate and I just smiled and said they should celebrate by themselves and she said was I sure and I said I was and she said she'd be home early and it's after eleven now and if you hear a car pull up you better tell me because if she sees me looking like this—"

"Wait a minute," Lee said. She got up and looked down at Virginia in the big armchair. "Why don't you tell her how you feel? Maybe it'll make a difference."

Virginia shook her head.

"How do you know?"

"Because I know. Because she said he's very kind, he cares about her a lot, he's pretty nice-looking, and he's rich. She and I won't have anything to worry about from now on. And if I have any bad feelings at all they'll go away when I see the suite they're giving me in their twenty-three room house."

"Wow."

"Yeah, wow. I'll tell you something, Lee . . . If you were the one telling me this story and I were standing right over there where you are, I'd be telling you you were crazy to be sitting there crying like an idiot. I'd say they're giving you a suite and you're crying, you crazy nut? I'd be the first to say that, you know?"

"I know." Lee smiled.

"Only it's me, not you, and I want to live with my

dad, not some stranger, and I don't care about any old suite, Lee, I really don't."

Lee said, "Yeah, I guess . . . Can you live with your dad?"

Virginia shook her head. "No. I already had the conversation with them in my head. My dad is gone all day and a lot of nights because he stays over at Sandy's. My mother really wants me to be with her and now she'll have the money so we'll both have the best kind of life. It's only logical that I stay with my mother. So I'll have to move to Connecticut, big deal. Lots of kids move and this is a good time to do it because I'm just starting high school."

"That's what they'll say," Lee agreed.

"Right? Sure, they will. Was that a car?"

"No, Gin. I still think you're better off telling your mother all this, though."

"Tell me, honestly, Lee. Do you think it would do one bit of good if I did?"

Lee said, "No."

"You see? So why bother?"

Lee shrugged. "Just to get it off your chest, that's all. Just to make them know you're around. I have to scream when I have to scream, Ginny, I always did, but that's me. You keep it inside and that's you. It doesn't even matter because in the end, it's just like Eileen said: we're shuffleboard people. All the adults decide what's best for us."

Virginia got up for another tissue. "You know, I got so into my own problem I didn't even ask you about what you said on the phone. Did you say you sneaked out of your mother's or something?"

Lee smacked her hand over her mouth. "Oh, no! I was going to call my father when I got here and I forgot. I just wanted to let him know I was okay and now it's probably too late . . ."

"Do you think they know you're missing?" Virginia asked.

"Probably not. You're right. My mother was dead to the world, she won't find out I'm gone till morning and by then I'll have called and that'll be it."

"What happened with your mother?" Virginia asked.

"Oh, I just blew up. Like I usually do . . . She's got this idea of a Lee in her head, but it's not the real one. She just doesn't—"

"—understand me," Virginia finished with her. "Believe me, I've been there."

"And I also said I wanted to live with my father. I told both of them, but they keep dodging me. I really think my father wants me, but I don't know what's going to happen . . ."

"Do you think your mother'd go to court to keep you?" Virginia asked matter-of-factly. "Do you think your father would?"

Lee shook her head. "I don't know," she said.

"It never came to that with any of us," Virginia said. "I hope it doesn't with you. Boy, that can get so—hey, was that a car?"

Lee turned and looked toward the living room

window. "Yeah, I see the lights in the driveway."

Virginia was up and racing for the bathroom. Lee found herself in the position of explaining her presence to Virginia's mother and her fiancé. Finally Virginia appeared with hair combed and fluffed, the red gone from her eyes and nose, and a welcoming smile on her glossed lips.

They heard about the Cornish game hen and wild rice her mother had had for dinner, about the quick drive to the city for a drink in a very special place that "Stewart" knew, for a stop at "Stewart's" New York apartment to pick up a few clothes and right back here to my baby, sorry I'm late.

Lee fell asleep on the couch, much to her embarrassment and Virginia's delight.

"Daddy?"

"Lee? Oh, my God, is that you, Lee?"

"I'm sorry I'm calling so late, Daddy, I overslept."

"Where are you? Do you have any idea how frantic your mother and I have been? She called me over two hours ago and I've been going out of my mind and so has she. *Where are you!*"

"Oh, Daddy, I'm at Virginia's, I was going to call you first thing and then I just overslept, I couldn't believe the time . . ."

"It's eleven-thirty.," her father said. "Virginia's? You're in town?"

"I took a train."

"By yourself? Why didn't you call me from the station?"

"Because I figured I'd get to you before you worried. I took a cab out here from the station and I'm glad I did because Virginia really needed me, Daddy—"

"Virginia needed you . . ."

"She really did."

"I'm hanging up to call your mother. You stay there, I'll call you right back."

Elaine Currie was huddled by the phone, the back of her fist in her mouth.

"It's okay, Elaine, she's at Virginia's. She took a train home and then a cab from the station. She just called, she overslept. Elaine? Elaine, are you there? Are you okay?"

"Thank God she's all right," she managed.

"What happened? No, never mind, don't even tell me. You had a stupid fight, right? No, sorry, Elaine, that was low . . ."

But she hadn't heard him. "Alan, I want to come out there," she said.

"Well . . . Okay . . . Why?"

"Why! Because I can't live this way, that's why! Because I've got to talk to my daughter, I don't want her to hate me, that's why! Alan?"

"Yeah, yeah, I'm here. Okay, Elaine, come on out."

Her mother arrived at the apartment an hour before Lee. When her father called Lee back, he'd prepared her that her mother would be coming out and offered to pick her up at Virginia's. Lee declined. She wanted to walk. She wanted to think.

Once home, she went to put her things in her room and avoided an instant confrontation with her mother and father, her brother and sister.

Finally, she walked into the living room and there they were: her mother in the chair; her father on the couch with Allison and Joel. All four of them were looking at her.

She looked back at them, but with her head lowered. "I'm sorry I worried you," she said. "I didn't mean to."

"You meant to when you walked out last night," her mother snapped. "What time did you leave?"

"Around nine-thirty."

"How did you think I would feel?" her mother asked, and Lee said, "How about the way *I* felt?" and her father said, "Stop it, both of you!"

Lee sat down on the floor.

"I think we should talk," her mother said quietly. "I know that none of us feels very good right now. Not about each other or about ourselves. Isn't that true?"

No one spoke. Lee began to trace the broad pattern in the rug with her finger. She really didn't want a fight. She felt so badly afterward, every time she hurt them . . .

"I'll start then," her mother said, and leaned forward on her chair. "Look, kids—your father and I aren't together any more and it's very hard on you. We know that, we knew it would be, but we're trying to do the best—we're trying to make the best of the situation. We don't know what else we can do."

Lee looked up at her. She thought, it's Mother who wants a fight. "You keep saying you want the best for us, only you're the ones who decide what's best, not us!"

Her mother started to answer, but Lee kept on. "You decided I should move my whole life around and come live with you in New York! Virginia's mother decides what they need is a rich husband, so Virginia has to move to Connecticut because that's best for her. Why do you think you always know what's best?"

"We don't," her father said calmly. "We don't. All we can do is try. And we have more experience, so there's more to base decisions on. They can be wrong decisions, Lee, but we're trying."

"What are you trying?" Lee asked. She turned to her mother. "Why do you want me to come and live with you, Mother? Is it because I'm so much fun to be around? Or because I can take some of the burden off Allison? Or because what would people think when your daughter isn't living with you?" She stopped because her mother's eyes were closed. "Why do you want me, Mother?"

"I don't know, Lee. I don't know why I should

want you. You jump on everything I say, you twist meanings, you don't listen to any advice I may have to offer you. I'm finally doing now something I've always wanted to do and you make me feel guilty and awful and all I get from you is disapproval."

Lee snorted.

"Oh, yes, I know, that's what you always say about *me*. But I do want you." Her mother's voice softened. "No, right now it's true: you're not a lot of fun to be around. And instead of taking off a burden, you'd be one. But I still want you.

"I knew splitting up would be hard. We all certainly know enough people who have gone through it. But one thing I didn't think of was—when you see your child for such brief periods of time—you think—at least *I* think—that I have to condense everything I ever planned to tell you, to teach you in just a few . . ."

Their father was nodding. "I know," he said. "I know. All your parental wisdom and caring and love—you have to get it all in on the telephone. Then you hang up and hope you covered everything because there's no next-morning-at-breakfast, or next-leisurely-evening-after-dinner. Even when you're together for the weekend, it's still—only a weekend."

"Yes . . ." their mother agreed. "And I don't want to miss your growing-up time, Lee. Even though you may not listen to a word I say, I just want to be there to say it . . ."

"Yeah," Lee cried, "you want to be there to say it, never mind if I want to hear it! Anyway, if you wanted to be there so badly, why did you get divorced in the first place?"

"Our divorce has nothing to do with the way your father and I feel about you. Both of us love you very much!"

"Bull!" Lee shouted and Joel jumped.

Neither of her parents cried "Lenore!" as she'd expected. No one said anything at all.

Lee glared at her mother. "You always thought you knew what was best for me, even when I didn't, and now that we hardly even see each other you still think so! You don't even know what's going on with me!"

"That's what I'm saying!" her mother sighed. "That's why I want you!"

"For you, not for me!"

"Wait," her father said quietly, holding up his hand. "It looks as though we're all pulling in separate directions, but what we have to remember is that the reason we're all having such a hard time is because we do love you. And you love us. The feelings your mother and I have for you three kids are and always will be our common bond. No divorce court can ever change that."

"I want to go back home!" Joel screamed. He turned to look at all of their faces and then he screamed again. "Why can't we just go home! To our old house! I want to go home!"

173

Allison began to grab for him, to put him on her lap to soothe him, but their father reached over and picked him up. "Listen, Joel," he said, holding him tightly, "there are times when we want something so badly we just can't imagine that we're not going to get it. We simply can't admit—" he touched Joel's chest, "—inside . . . that our wish won't come true. It's like trying to make our own magic, by saying things like, 'If I don't step on any cracks in the sidewalk on my way to school then I'll get an A in Math.' Or, 'If I remember to get out of bed on the left side instead of the right, then I'll have a good day all day.' Joelly, you want it all to be the way it was for you before, you want it so badly that you keep thinking about it as if it could happen. You have to let go of it, Joel, because it can't." He stroked his son's hair. "I can promise you that things will get better. And easier. But it won't be the way it was, Joel . . ."

Joel began to cry softly.

"Soon school will start," their father continued. "You'll have a new and exciting time. And then we'll set up a regular visiting schedule again and you'll have a real routine . . ."

"Get used to it, Joelly," Lee said. "Nothing lasts. Mother'll get married again and Daddy will and all of us will have another new life! And then maybe they'll be divorced again!"

"Lenore! That's a horrible thing to say!"

"Well, I'm sorry, but isn't it true? No relationship

lasts, look at us, and look at me, I can't even keep a boyfriend for a month!" There were tears in her eyes but she didn't care. "Nothing lasts at all!" she repeated.

Allison hadn't spoken a word. She stood up suddenly. "I want to go back, to New York," she said. "I want to go now."

They turned to her, surprised. As usual, her calm presence had been taken for granted. Lee, the vocal one, commanded the attention. Feeling this, her father was ashamed. He reached out a hand to her. "Allie, come here . . ." he began.

Allison drew back with a gasp. "No!" she cried, shocking them all, herself included.

"Allie . . ."

"I'm sorry," she whispered. "I'm tired. I just want to go."

Her parents looked at each other.

"I guess I'll take them back," their mother said quietly and stood.

"Well . . . look . . . How about staying here at least for dinner?" their father suggested but he didn't insist when she shook her head.

Lee got up and faced her mother. "I'm staying here," she said quietly but emphatically. "I'm not going to New York to live. I'm staying. Right, Daddy?" Defiantly she looked up at her father.

"I want you to stay," he said, nodding, but he was looking at her mother.

Lee's heart turned over. She stepped outside

quickly, wanting to hug the moment and not wanting to hear its aftermath.

"I could go to court, you know," her mother said softly when Lee had left.

"And so could I. Things have changed, Elaine. Fathers have rights, in case you haven't noticed. There are no guarantees either way, but what's always been done isn't 'always' any more."

"We'll see. Where's Allison?"

"On her way to the car with Joel. Come on, I'll drive you to the station."

Lee joined them in the car for the ride. No one spoke, and no one really looked at each other. Joel's voice from the back of the car startled them.

"Look," he said, pointing. "There's our house . . ."

Their father didn't look. He passed it every day on his way to the station. It had ceased to be his house, he never gave it a thought. Now he did.

It was always too big, their mother thought. It was a lot of work. But there were some nice times. I remember when we bought it . . . Lenore was two. That day we went to look at it for the first time, she had a diaper rash and cried and cried—even when I showed her the big back yard . . .

It's just a house, Allison thought. It's not ours. It's only a house, it doesn't mean anything . . .

Maybe someday I'll have a house like it, Lee thought. We'll never live there again, but maybe someday I'll make a family for a house like that. Maybe . . .

"Allison? Are you awake?"

"Yes . . ."

"May I come in for a minute?"

"Okay."

Her mother sat down on Allison's bed. "You hardly said a single word today, at your father's . . ."

Allison didn't answer.

"I wondered . . . what you were thinking."

Allison rolled over on her back and her mother could see her eyes in the light from the hall.

"Allison?"

"I hate him," Allison whispered.

"What?"

"I hate Daddy sometimes!" She pulled herself up. "He left us, he left all of us and I hate him!"

Frightened, her mother held Allison's arms. "Honey, he didn't walk out on us, you know what happened—"

"But he left!" She began to cry.

"Oh, Allison!" She pulled her close.

Allison was sobbing now. "I didn't mean it," she said. "I really don't hate Daddy. I love him."

"I know."

"I love him . . ." Allison repeated and rested her cheek against her mother's shoulder.

Twelve

Ten days later, Elaine Currie came directly to the WNVL offices without phoning ahead. She skipped one of her classes to be there early.

Alan Currie wasn't there. He was putting Sally Post on an early morning plane to Albany. There was traffic on the way back into Manhattan, so the approximate arrival time he'd given to his secretary was an hour off.

She was pacing the hall when he stepped off the elevator and saw her.

"Alan!" she began. He took her arm, guided her into his office and closed the door.

She opened her purse and took out a piece of paper." "I've gotten some recommendations for therapists for Allison from by boss and some people at school. If you want to check on them, here's the list. I already have and they're all highly qualified. If there's anyone else you feel would be—"

"No. If you say they're okay, then fine. We'll go ahead." Then he asked, "How is she? When I saw her last week she was very quiet. But I couldn't tell—"

"It doesn't get any better," she said. She rubbed her forehead to ease the tension she felt behind her eyes. "She worries so. Especially about Joel, but about everything. She talks about hating us. We can't—*I* can't handle it myself."

"Don't worry about it. We'll do it together. The sooner the better."

"By the way, your insurance covers this. Mine doesn't yet. I checked."

"We'd afford it regardless, Elaine."

"I know . . ."

He stood straighter. "Elaine, is there something else you want to tell me?"

"I'm not going to court, Alan."

"I'm glad to hear it."

"Oh, Alan, you knew I wouldn't fight you. I couldn't force her to come."

"There are all kinds of force, Elaine, not just through a judge."

"Yes."

"I would have hated fighting you for Lee—in court or in private. But I would have. A few weeks ago I didn't know that. Anyway, I believe it's best for her to be with me at this time, and she does, too. She knew it all along."

"But I'll miss being there for her. And with Allison now—"

He leaned against his desk. "She was so terrific before. When we were together, she was the . . . well, the glue of the family. Calm, rational, giving . . ."

"Don't do that, Alan," she said and touched his arm. "We don't really know what would have happened. Maybe Allison was always too controlled. Maybe we would have gone on taking her for granted and paying no attention until something else happened to upset her world."

"Maybe . . . maybe . . ."

"It would be harder on Lee to live with us . . . But they need us both. Still. They need as much support as they can get—from both of us."

He nodded. Long after she left he still felt her words. Support from both of us. All of them. Always.

Lee slammed the door loudly. "I'm home!" she yelled.

"How could I miss it?" her father called from the kitchen. "Why are you so late?"

"There were tryouts! For *The Music Man!* Eileen and I stayed to audition!" She dropped her books and stood in the kitchen doorway. "We didn't want a part or anything, but it would be fun to be in the chorus. Mr. Abrams is the director and he's nice."

"What'll you do if you get a part?"

"Take it, of course! But I won't get one. I can't sing loud. Did you ask Sally?"

"Ask her what?"

"Daddy, you said this morning you were going to invite Sally for the weekend. Didn't you? Or did I hear wrong?"

"Well, I wanted to talk to you about it first."

"Why? I can be very discreet. Lock myself in my room from Friday night to Sunday . . ."

"You don't have to lock yourself anywhere—"

"Or I could go to Eileen's. Even Ginny's, although her house is full of cartons and boxes—"

"I don't want you to go *anywhere*," he said emphatically. "I want you right here."

"You want me to get used to seeing her around."

"Is it going to embarrass you or make you uncomfortable if Sally stays here?"

"No."

"The truth?"

"Of course not! I'm a big girl, Daddy. Don't forget, Eileen had Howard sleeping over at her place since she was—"

"This is us, Lee, not your friend. I really need to know how you feel."

"Fine."

"I don't believe you."

Lee reddened. "Well . . . I guess I feel kind of funny. Part of me knows that it's perfectly natural, I mean, you are a grown man . . . And I know you like Sally. I've gotten to like her, too . . ."

"Have you?"

"Are you going to marry her?"

"Honey, all we want to do is see each other a lot and find out if what we feel is really what it seems to be and if it is then we'll keep feeling it and if it isn't then it wasn't and we won't."

Lee giggled. "You won't believe this, but I understood that."

"I know!"

"I'm not used to you having . . . to you being . . ." She stopped and smiled. "But that's all it is, Daddy. I'm just not used to you being somebody's boyfriend. . . . But I'll get used to it because I know that it won't change what you feel for me."

He put down the batter he had been stirring. "Do you really know that?" he asked, turning to face her.

"I really do. I feel better about a lot of things since I knew I was going to stay here permanently."

He nodded. "I've noticed that."

"I have this thing. With Mother."

"I noticed that, too," he said ruefully.

"No, but—I see it better now. Remember that family conference we had? After I ran away? I wanted to walk home, remember?"

"From Virginia's. I remember."

"I thought about how every time I'm with Mother I end up fighting with her. And I didn't want to that day. I was sorry I hurt her. I'm always sorry but I can't help it. I made up my mind while I was walking home that no matter what happened when I got here I wouldn't fight with her any more. And I still did. It's like a pattern," she continued. "I don't do it with you . . . It's like I need to fight with her."

"You do, I guess," her father said. "You bounce your frustrations off her to find out if she really loves you. She does, you know."

"I guess . . ."

"Mom needs to confront you, too, with what she wants for you, what she has to give you. Maybe it'll always be like that for you. Or maybe you'll feel secure enough some day so that 'Mother being Mother' won't bother you so much. I honestly don't know . . ."

"Anyway, I'm glad I'm here," Lee said and smiled.

"Me, too," he said. "I hope things work out as well for your sister."

"I bet they will, now that she's seeing Dr. Pushbutton."

"Cut that out, it's Puschmetter. And he's supposed to be good. Specializes in teen-age problems."

"Of which there are many . . ."

"Of which there are many. It's only been a few weeks, but I feel good knowing we have someone professional we can lean on instead of our own poorly equipped selves."

"Poor Daddy."

"No, no. Not 'poor Daddy.' I have you and Joel and Allison and you've all got me and your mother. No matter where we all live, even when you're grown."

"It scares me though," she said, "that you make all these plans in your life and they just may all get wrecked." She went to the sink to help him. He handed her an onion and the grater.

"You're right, it's scary. Your plans and expectations could fall apart. You just have to be careful not to fall apart with them. If you look carefully, you might find something good in the wreck." He looked over at her and gasped. "Like that onion you're grating into the tapioca pudding!"

"Oh, no! I thought it was soup!"

"How could you think tapioca pudding was *soup?*"

"I don't know, but maybe it'll turn out to be good. Just as you said."

"You mean 'make the best out of the situation'?"

"Yeah . . ."

They looked into the bowl and then up at each other.

"Are you putting on weight?" she asked.

"A little," he said and smiled. "Are you?"

"A lot."

"So we won't have dessert."

They met at the beach for purely sentimental reasons; the weather was not obliging. It was cool for September, especially near the ocean. They all wore sweaters and kept pushing their wind-blown hair out of their faces.

"Thanks, Eileen," Virginia said.

"What for?"

"For my 'farewell party,' dummy, what else?"

"Oh, Gin, it's not a farewell party, we're not saying goodbye to you. It's just the four of us being together again until . . . next time, that's all."

"Still, it's nice to get out of my house. My mother's behaving like a twelve year old," Virginia said.

"It's too bad you've got to start school late up there," Connie said. "I mean, just by a few weeks."

"No, I want to stay here as long as I can," Virginia said. "I guess that sounds silly . . ."

"You know, the weird thing is," Eileen said, "I thought we'd be having a sad little gathering like this for Lee, not Ginny."

"That's right," Lee said. "I was the one who was supposed to be leaving. That was the plan all summer. And it got changed at the last minute."

Virginia sighed. "Yeah, and my plan all summer was to stay right here and *that* got changed at the last minute."

"That's what my father and I talked about," Lee said. "Plans can get wrecked but sometimes that's good. This time it was good for me and bad for Gin."

"Well, maybe it will be good for Gin, too," Connie said. "Maybe she'll love her new place."

Virginia said, "Yeah. Sure."

"Well," Connie added, "your social life was dead, maybe it'll pick up there."

"Speaking of social lives, I saw Warren the other day," Lee said. "Just real quick, as he was going into the cafeteria."

"Did you talk to him?" Eileen asked.

"Oh, no, he didn't see me. My stomach still turned over but then I was okay. I could even concentrate on my French class."

"Well, things aren't going that great between Buff and me now, either," Eileen said. "I guess it was just one of those summer things."

"Why?"

"Oh, I don't know—he's got band a few times a week, I've got *Music Man* rehearsals, he's working, I'm visiting my father—it's logistics. We just don't have time."

"You don't seem so broken up about it," Connie said.

"I'm not, I guess. Couldn't tell you why, though . . . Unless maybe he looks cuter in a bathing suit than in his band sweater." She giggled. "It looks so 'high school.' "

"Things sure turned around," Virginia said, shaking her head. "All different from just a few weeks ago . . ." She touched Lee's hand. "At least things are working out for you, though, Lee. I'm really glad about that."

Lee's eyes filled with tears. "It'll work out for you, too, Gin," she said. "I know it will. And besides, with such a big house, you can easily have your three friends visiting you and we won't even get in any-one's way!"

"That's right!" Eileen cried. "We can each have our own wing!"

"Oh, hey," Virginia said, "I feel better already. What about next weekend?"

"Ohhh, I'm with my father."

"Me, too."

"Oh, boy, here we go again!"

"No," Lee said. "We'll make the time. There always has to be time for people you love." She held up her can of Diet Pepsi. "Here's to the Shuffleboard Four! We'll stay together!"

The other three soda cans clinked against hers. "Here, here!" three voices cried against the wind.

About the Author

Judie Angell has written seven novels for young people: *Ronnie and Rosey, Tina Gogo, Secret Selves, In Summertime It's Tuffy, A Word from Our Sponsor or My Friend Alfred, Dear Lola or How to Build Your Own Family,* and *What's Best for You.* Before publishing her first book, in 1977, she taught elementary school, wrote promotion copy for Channel 13, New York City's educational television station, and did editorial work for *TV Guide.*

Judie Angell lives with her husband, a musician, and their two sons in a house on a lake in South Salem, New York.